SLOWGRIND

SLOWGRIND

GAY MEN TELL THEIR
REAL-LIFE SEX STORIES

edited by
AUSTIN FOXXE

alyson books
los angeles | new york

MANUFACTURED IN THE UNITED STATES OF AMERICA.

THIS TRADE PAPERBACK ORIGINAL IS PUBLISHED BY ALYSON PUBLICATIONS.
P.O. BOX 4371, LOS ANGELES, CA 90078-4371.
DISTRIBUTION IN THE UNITED KINGDOM BY TURNAROUND PUBLISHER SERVICES LTD.,
UNIT 3, OLYMPIA TRADING ESTATE, COBURG ROAD, WOOD GREEN,
LONDON N22 6TZ ENGLAND.

FIRST EDITION: JULY 2000

00 01 02 03 04 **a** 10 9 8 7 6 5 4 3 2 1

ISBN 1-55583-560-0

LIBRARY OF CONGRESS CATALOGING-IN-PUBLICATION DATA
  SLOW GRIND : GAY MEN TELL THEIR REAL-LIFE SEX STORIES / EDITED BY
AUSTIN FOXXE.—1ST ED.
    ISBN 1-55583-560-0
    1. GAY MEN—SEXUAL BEHAVIOR. I. FOXXE, AUSTIN.
  HQ76.556 2000
  306.76'62—DC21   00-029282

COVER PHOTOGRAPHY BY JOHNATHAN BLACK.
COVER DESIGN BY PHILIP PIROLO.

The Alley off Polk Street by Michael Marsh   1

Canceled Flight by Steve Attwood   9

Champagne Surprise by Jeff Fisher   17

Friendly Couple by Donovan Lee   22

Night Maneuvers by Jason Di Giulio   27

The Call by Shaun Levin   37

Sunday Morning by Wes Berlin   44

The Challenge by Jeff Fisher   48

The Driver by A.J. Arvveson   54

Underwear Night at Charlie's by Peter Paul Sweeney   65

The Gold Cock Ring by B.B. Wills   72

The Handyman by Trevor J. Callahan Jr.   77

Out of the Closet by William Holden   86

Getting It Straight by Bob Condron   96

Paradise Falls by B.B. Wills   104

Love in the Midnight Sun by Kevin J. Olomon   110

Cool Shirt by A.J. Arvveson   119

Showy Joey by Ryan Field   128

The Woodsman by Lee Nichols   141

Finally Friday by Edgar Wayne   150

Score! by B.B. Wills   157

Remembering Richard by Andy Ohio   162

Horsing Around by Gareth MacKenzie   171

YMCA by Sean L. Avery   178

Anything by mike mazur   185

Contributor Biographies   193

The Alley off Polk Street

Michael Marsh

I spot the parking place and the hustler at the same time. He lounges there, one leg propped up against the crude graffiti on the brick wall. At the sound of my car he turns his head, smiles, and looks straight at me, the expression on his face expectant and mildly curious. I notice his eyes first, dark sparkling eyes framed by equally dark lashes. His crown of long jet-black hair is brushed back into a ponytail. It shines as it catches the warm October sunlight. *My God!* I think, *he is wonderful; he is sexy.* My body suddenly shivers with lust.

I am instantly aware of how different he is from the general population of homeless youth who meander up and down Polk Street daily. He is young, somewhere in his 20s, I suppose. He is well-built, of medium height, his body slender and lean. Nothing about it is pronounced. He has no tattoos, no pierced body parts that I can see, no buff biceps or triceps, no rounded melon buttocks or bulging basket so beloved of gay fantasy. Rather, his are the radiant, handsome American good looks of a healthy young boy out for an afternoon of adventure, preferably naughty. His white T-shirt and faded blue jeans hang loosely on his frame. He wears white socks and decrepit sneakers, their soles held in place with electrical duct tape. I laugh at the sneakers. When I was at Princeton I wrapped mine the same way. Looking at him, I have only one thought: *I must have this beautiful boy!*

As I pull into the parking place, he strolls up to the car and leans casually on the frame of the open passenger window.

"Hi, my name is Christian." His smile is open, friendly, almost bashful.

"Christian? That's an imposing name."

"Yeah. It's my dad's name too. My folks call me Chrissy, but around here, I'm usually just Kit."

"Kit's easier; it suits you," I comment. "Hi, Kit. I'm Michael."

"What do you know," he remarks. "My first boyfriend's name was Michael. Nice car, Michael," he says, looking at the interior. "What year is it?"

"It's a 1968," I answer. "Twenty years old last month."

"Classic." Clearly, Kit likes my car. "A real beauty. Do you mind if I get in for a minute? I've never sat in a Mercedes before," he says as he opens the door, taking his invitation for granted.

"I'm not sure how to say this," I say, struggling to hide my nervousness. "Are you working, Kit?"

"You bet," comes his cheerful answer. "But before we go any further I have to ask: Are you a policeman?"

"Of course not!" Panic seizes me. "What in the world makes you ask me a question like that?"

"Oh, there are cops out here almost every day busting us, but in California they're not allowed to lie about it—at least they're not supposed to anyway, so it's just something that has to be asked up front," Kit explains. "So, Michael, what's on your mind?"

My anxiety is real. For a moment I am embarrassed, at a loss for words.

"I don't know. This is the first time I've ever done anything like this—picked up someone on the street like this, I mean." I struggle for composure. "I suppose I need to find out how much this costs," I say to avoid Kit's question. "I mean, is there a standard rate? Or does it vary?"

"Forty dollars," comes the prompt answer. "Do you have a place where we can go? What do you like to do, Michael?"

There is the question again. I swallow hard. *God, he's so hot, but can I really do this?* I ask myself. Finally, the words spill out. "I want to be naked with you. I want to suck you. I like to be sucked, but most of all I want to be fucked." There, I've said it.

"OK," Kit smiles. "But just in case you're wondering, I only have safe sex, and I don't let anybody fuck me. Everything else is just fine, so let's go." With that he sinks back into the camel-colored leather seat, prepared to enjoy his ride in a classic car.

We swing out into the traffic on Larkin Street. "I only live a few blocks away, off Sacramento, so it isn't much of a ride," I apologize.

"That's OK. It's fun even if it's short."

"Do you mind if I ask: Are you gay? Or do you do this with men and women?"

"Queer as a $3 bill," Kit answers. "Always have been. As far as women are concerned, I guess you could say I'm still a virgin."

"Well, do you have any particular rules about your work? I mean, besides having safe sex."

"Yeah, sure there are, a few. I never go with anyone driving a van. Vans scare me. And I never go with more than one man at a time unless I already know one of them. A threesome can be fun with one of my regular dates but not with strangers. Too many hustlers get beaten up going out with two guys at once. Getting fucked just hurts. I don't like it."

I turn the car into the garage of my building. We get out and start toward the elevator.

"I do have one more rule," Kit adds. "Not that it applies to us, but I won't go out with a guy who asks me 'How big is it?' the very first thing. It just pisses me off; it's so rude. When I get asked 'How big is it' the very first thing, I usually say 'Fuck off, asshole! You want the biggest dick west of the Mississippi, go down to the porno house on Jones Street and jerk off with the stars, man!' That's really pretty much everything."

We ride the elevator and walk down the hallway in silence. "Here we are," I say as I fish through my pockets for my keys. We walk into the living room. "Would you like a drink, Kit?" I offer.

"Sure. Scotch if you have some."

I start to pour the whisky into a pair of old-fashioned crystal glasses.

"Do you take anything in your drink?" I ask.

"Just some ice cubes and a splash of water, thanks."

I finish making our drinks, pick them up, and hand one to Kit. "Let's take these into the bedroom with us." My throat is dry, my voice husky.

"OK," he agrees, following me.

I set my glass on my bedside table and start to take off my clothes. My hands fumble with my shirt buttons. Goddamn it! I jerk off my shirt, throw it on the floor, kick out of my loafers, unbuckle my belt, yank my boxers and my khakis down together in one motion, then bend down to tug myself free from the legs. Naked at last, I am so nervous I almost fall on the foot of the bed facing my date.

In contrast to my struggle, Kit goes about the business of undressing slowly, with casual ease. He sets his drink on the chest of drawers, peels his T-shirt over his head, folds it neatly, and sits down in a wing chair to unlace his shoes and take off his socks. That task complete, he removes a couple of plastic-wrapped condoms and a small tube of lubricant from his pocket and tosses them on the bed. He turns to the mirror behind him, removes the band from his ponytail, and shakes out his ebony mane. I sit there, transfixed by the delicate spray of freckles across his shoulders. Still facing the mirror, he shucks off his jeans, then turns to face me, wearing only his white briefs, the suggestion of a smile hovering at the corners of his mouth.

He is so young, so beautiful. I tremble as I sit there, my erection aching, a thin film of moisture covering my nakedness. I reach out with both arms. "Come here, please," I whisper.

Quietly, Kit walks to me. I cup his buttocks with my hands, draw him closer, kneading his solid flesh. As if hypnotized by the outline of his sex, I bury my face in the soft, warm white jersey and start to lick it. He ruffles my hair with one hand, a gentle gesture. He stands there passively, submitting to me. At last he pulls down his underwear, releasing his penis. It springs out above Kit's tight, leathery sac and sable pubic hair, swollen and bursting with life, out of its fabric prison, slapping my face, slapping his belly. A whiff of sweet, soap-fresh musky perfume, his intimate smell, fills my nostrils. Desire overwhelms me.

"Do you like my cock, Michael?" I hear Kit's voice, softly, as if from some distant place. "Do you like my balls? Lick my balls, Michael. Gently...gently, now, Michael...lick me...yes, that's good, Michael...that's right...oh, that's great...keep on, Michael...oh, yes, that's great...I love to have my balls licked." Mindlessly, I follow his directions.

"Now, lick under my balls, that's right, long licks, make me wet, Michael…oh, that's good, Michael…you're making my cock really hard…look at it…that's right. See how hard you've made me? Now open your mouth, and take me down your throat, take me down your throat, Michael, yeah, that's right…open your mouth, Michael…don't move, just take me…that's it, that's it…Oh, God, Michael!" Kit grasps my hair and the back of my neck with his hands, holding my head helpless in his grip. His cock engulfs my mouth, and I devour him. I reel from the taste. The flavor is rich and salty and sweet. I feast on Kit's penis like someone being rescued from the brink of starvation. Suddenly, he withdraws, releasing himself.

"Look at my cock, Michael. Look how hard you've made me, look how wet and red and hard I am. I'm going to fuck you now. That's what you want, isn't it? Do you want to be fucked, Michael? Tell me…tell me."

"Yes, please," I plead. "Please!"

"Lie back on the bed." Kit's voice is firm, commanding. "Put some pillows behind your head…be comfortable, Michael…that's right…relax." He hands me a condom. "Help me with this. You have to help me get ready to fuck you. Roll it on my cock…that's the way…roll it on so I can fuck you. Kit reaches behind my knees and hoists my legs over his shoulders. He begins to lubricate me with first one finger and then two. "You have a nice ass, Michael…relax…this is what you want, isn't it? Isn't it, Michael? This is what you've been waiting for. I'm going to fuck your ass…now, Michael…*now.*" Kit takes complete possession of me with one direct thrust. I feel no pain. Rather, I am consumed by some primal pleasure. Kit rides me, alternating slow massaging strokes and teasing jabs. When I can bear it no longer, I seize my own erection and start to masturbate.

Kit sweeps away my hand. "No, Michael. Let me do that. I'm here to give you pleasure. Do you want to come, Michael? Do you want to shoot your load? Do you want to come with my cock inside you? Shoot, Michael, shoot your load. I want you to come while I'm fucking you. I want to feel you. His voice becomes more emphatic as he urges me on. Come…do it, Michael…shoot…shoot your load while I'm fucking your ass…do it, Michael…do it…*do it!*" Kit shouts his command.

I am frenzied by Kit's voice. He slathers me with lubricant. He holds me erect at the base of my cock and strokes the length of my shaft. I start to whimper, then make grunting, growling noises. My back arches in my effort to grind us together. As I feel my climax begin I involuntarily start to reject Kit's penis. I can't help it.

"Don't push me out, Michael," he cries. But I do. It's beyond my control. I see myself ejaculate before I feel the spasm of my orgasm, as a single great burst arcs over my head. I do not hear my scream. I do hear Kit cry out, "Oh, fuck…oh, fuck!" Then, quietly, "I'm going to come." I watch him pump his swollen penis, now freed from its latex sheath. His orgasm erupts, again and again, splashing my stomach, my chest, my face. Still grasping his sex, Kit falls on top of me, quivering spastically. We lay there, fused to one another, until the excitement subsides.

"Jesus Christ!"

I hear Kit's voice, but I'm too exhausted to respond.

He rouses himself, rolls over onto his back, and stretches.

"Goddamn, Michael! I hope your neighbors haven't called the police. You do make a noise."

"Do I? I didn't know it."

"That was some yell," he teases me.

"Well," I answer, "that was some fuck. Thank you."

"We both need a shower. You're covered, mister."

"OK. In a minute." I reach out for my khakis, rummage through the pockets for my cigarettes, extract one, and light it. I drag the acrid smoke deep into my lungs.

"Nothing is better than a cigarette after sex," I remark.

"You shouldn't smoke. Cigarettes are bad for you."

"Well, there you go," I reply. I take another drag, unwilling to let go of the sight of this beautiful naked boy beside me, his penis now only slightly swollen and at rest.

"Mellors called his cock John Thomas," I say idly.

"What?" Kit looks puzzled.

"Mellors called his cock John Thomas."

"I don't get it."

"Mellors was a character in a novel. He had this wonderful cock, and he really knew what to do with it. The way you do. He called his cock John Thomas," I explain. "I was just looking at you and the thought came into my head.

"Was he gay?" Kit asks.

"Not even a little bit."

"Oh," Kit shrugs, losing interest. "May I take that shower now?

"May I come too?"

"Sure. If you want to."

When we are freshly scrubbed and fully dressed, we walk out to the living room, and I make us fresh drinks.

"This has been nice, Michael," Kit says.

"I think so too." I extract two $20 bills from my money clip, add another $10 for good measure, and hand them over. Kit just tucks the money into his pocket without counting it.

"I mean it," he says. "This has been really nice. Maybe we can get together again sometime."

"Maybe—"

It was ten years ago that I turned into that alley looking for a parking place. Today is our anniversary.

Canceled Flight

Steve Attwood

I'm normally a happy-go-lucky sort of guy with an unsinkable sense of humor and a ready smile for anyone, but on the day I met Aaron, I was in a really foul mood. My head pounded with pain, and my shoulders hunched with the tension that comes from accumulated, unrelieved stress. I couldn't have felt less sexy if I tried.

It had been a tough week in Wellington, the capital city of New Zealand, and the site of a lot of head offices for various departments of the government, including my own Department of Conservation. I was normally stationed at Hokitika, on the wild and isolated west coast of South Island. A quarter of New Zealand's protected wilderness is in that region, so my job was important, but it was a place where life was laid-back and the pace not hectic.

I'd been called to headquarters to stand in for our media manager while he was on extended leave. I had to do his work and still try to manage, from a distance, the media and public information program for my own region.

Still, there had been some compensation for being in the hustle and bustle of the capital rat race: The gay scene in Wellington was always exciting. Friendly, outrageous, and proud of its visibility, Wellington was a world away from the rural conservative air of Hokitika, where gays were almost all closeted and invisible; there was no such thing as a gay bar or even a private club or contact group.

I was being hosted by my employers in the heart of the capital's accommodation, restaurant, and entertainment district, and my nights were as long as my days but much more pleasurable. There was the excitement of meeting and fucking new men or finding old friends in the crowd for unexpected reunions where the sex had a special, nostalgic quality.

But burning the candle at both ends had taken its toll. I was physically and sexually exhausted and intellectually burned out. All I wanted was to get home, to my own bed—alone! And that was causing the frustration. After a wild and bumpy flight from Wellington on a Friday afternoon, I was stranded, halfway home, at Christchurch, on the opposite side of the South Island from where I was supposed to be. My connecting flight on a small commuter plane to Hokitika had been grounded by the same storm that had made my flight from the capital such a rough journey. Even for the big planes, flying conditions were marginal, and it was understandable that my flight, which traversed New Zealand's highest mountains, where the storm would be at its most fierce, had to be canceled. My understanding the reasons didn't make up for the inconvenience and frustration.

Fuck, that's all I bloody need, I thought. *A weekend in Christchurch with nowhere to stay and no bloody money.* Because I had been anticipating a quiet weekend at home and normal work routine the following week, I had blown almost all my spending money living it up in Wellington. To top it off, the airline had lost one of my bags, the one with all my best clothes, the stuff I liked to wear outside work when cruising bars, restaurants, and gay venues.

A phone call to my secretary got me the name of a hotel where the DOC had an account, which meant I didn't have to pay for the room or charge it to my at-its-limit credit card. I figured I had just enough cash to scrape through the next 48 hours. After checking in I phoned the airport and asked to have my bag delivered to my hotel if it was found, though I didn't hold out much hope.

Exhausted, I hung up the do not disturb sign, shut the door, stripped, and crashed naked onto the freshly made bed with its clean, cool sheets. Sleep came quickly but not for long. I awoke hungry and horny. Amazingly, my energy had returned and with it my natural good spirits, aided by the fact that as I had slept, room service had dropped off my missing bag, found and delivered to the hotel by the airport.

Shit, I thought, *if I'm going to be stuck in the city, I might as well enjoy myself.* I had a shower and while drying myself checked out my bod in the full-length mirror. At 39, I was starting to worry about being unattached. Mr. Right had proved elusive. I was still self-confident enough to appreciate the assets I had: My hair, though graying, was thick, shiny, and naturally curled; my body was in good shape from hiking through the valleys and mountains of the national park that backed onto Hokitika; my chest was thick with black hair that narrowed as it trailed down my stomach and flared out into a forest just before plunging below my belly button into a thick crop of glossy curls around my cock.

I cupped my balls, warmed by the hot shower and hanging like large plums in their extended sac, and lifted them to my cock, which was achingly erect. I have a generous foreskin, which pulled back away from the flaring glans as I stroked my desire, precome glistening in my cock's single eye. I have to admit, I liked the weight and the look of my equipment, and no one had ever complained it was too small.

You can wait, I told my throbbing member. Anticipation is the best aphrodisiac I know.

I dressed quickly. I turned the silver in my hair to my advantage, highlighting the natural color scheme with a lustrous black silk shirt that clung to my fairly hefty frame and a silver dragon pendant emphasizing the valley between my pecs. This was teamed with a silver earring, watch, and bracelet. Black jeans and black boots with silver trim completed the look.

Women and men turned to look at me as I crossed the hotel lobby. I felt hot.

After a few drinks at No Names, which was the gay bar in Christchurch at the time (it's closed now), I decided to cruise to Men Friends, a gay sauna and cruise club. It was there that I met Aaron.

He was young and wrapped only in a towel. He sauntered into the reception area from the sauna room just as I was buzzed through the security door. It wasn't something I normally did, turn on to young guys; I'd sort of made up my mind that Mr. Right was probably going to be about my age. This time it was different; magic sparked through the air. From the moment our eyes met, desire flowed like ribbons of energy between us. Aaron was 23 and wore his dark hair cut close at the sides and spiky—almost unruly—across the crown. His gray-green eyes, glowing with barely subdued energy, were framed by long, almost feminine, lashes. As he moved, the musculature of true manhood was evident, just beginning to emerge through the slenderness of youth. What I liked most about him was his blatant and unapologetic cruising. He just stood there, grinning, holding my gaze, enjoying the progress of my eyes over his body. I cast one more long, meaningful glance and headed for the cruise maze and bunk rooms, praying this sexy young man would follow.

In the dim maze I was almost invisible in my black outfit, but even so, other hopefuls crowded against me, touching my ass, my basket, my tits, hoping I'd choose them. But I wasn't interested; I had eyes only for the youth who'd held my gaze at the reception area. I looked around as I desperately tried to pick his profile from the shadows of other occupants of the maze. There he was. He had followed.

"You want some company tonight?" It sounded corny, but it was all I could think of to say. In a voice with a deep timbre that belied his years, the youth gave a reply that made me feel giddy.

"I've been wanting you to ask that since you came in." Aaron followed actions with words, grasping my hand and pulling me into the nearest bunk room. We fell into a deep embrace, lips and hips locked in grinding passion, tongues probing, hot mouths sucking and chewing, breath almost instantly ragged, gasping, filled with desire. In seconds I was naked, my clothes joining the youth's towel in an untidy bundle on the floor. Aaron followed the last item down, sliding to his knees as he drew my briefs past my towering erection and down over my legs, helping me step out of them. I gasped as his hot mouth closed on my aching cock. He was good—*damned* good. From tip to bush, my cock slid in and out of Aaron's willing mouth. Even in the dimness of the room, I could see the youth's slim throat expand to accommodate each deeply penetrating thrust. Aaron murmured with contentment as he reached up to run his hands through my thick chest hair until his nimble fingers found the thick, pouty nipples crowning each broad, flat pec.

"Tits from heaven," he sighed as he began to tweak, pinch, and pull without once ceasing his mouth-fucking. I could feel the come boiling in my balls, then my knees buckled as the first powerful surges of erotic heat burst from my loins and exploded up my belly and across my chest.

"A-a-ah, I'm coming," I warned, and Aaron slipped his mouth off my extended organ and went down on my balls instead, sucking furiously as my come burst free. The hot semen fell onto the youth's face and sprinkled his hair, filling the air with the intense smell of hot man juice. Bending down, I cupped my heavy arms around Aaron's buttocks and lifted him to my waist. Instinctively he wrapped his legs about me, tucking his ass and balls in tight against my mat of pubic hair.

"O-o-oh, fuck me, big man, fuck me," Aaron pleaded, squirming and grinding against my cock, which was already beginning to return to full erection. My fingers found the cleavage between the youth's buttocks and dove deep, probing a hole that was as warm and moist as any pussy and just as willing for a big cock to fill it.

Placing Aaron on his back on the edge of the bunk, I lifted his legs over my shoulders, slipped on a condom from the supply provided in each cubicle, and opened a sachet of lube from the same source.

"You're gonna get your wish lad," I growled, roughly fingering the puckered ass that was being lifted up to me. "Damn, you're hot and ready," I exclaimed as not one but three fingers slipped inside to find the swollen love gland hidden there. I replaced my fingers with cock, shoving deep and fast as I lifted Aaron from the bed, pulling his hips up and forward to meet my surging manhood. Aaron screamed with pleasure and clinched my cock with his hot ass muscles, milking the swollen tool that filled his every desire. Sweat dripped from my forehead and chest to mingle with Aaron's own fluids as our lovemaking reached its crescendo. We screamed, yelled, and swore hard-fucking expletives of love and passion to each other as our joint climaxes built. Then we exploded together into orgasm, coming in shuddering gasps and groans that were heard throughout the maze. I learned later that guys outside were jacking off in the corridors, turned on just by the noise of our extended passion.

For long minutes we lay silent, hugging in each other's warmth as the heat of passion faded into the comfortable glow that follows great sex. And then we talked quietly, learning about each other, lust quickly being replaced by the first hints of love. Minutes passed into an hour, and talking stopped as passion returned.

"Fuck me," I whispered into my young lover's ear. "I want to feel your hard cock deep inside me." Aaron was amazed. He liked older, hairy guys like me, but they always did the fucking. He told me his cock had never felt the velvet insides of a man.

I grinned. "That's fitting," I told him. "Virgin cock for a virgin ass. I've never been fucked before, but I want yours, and I want it now." Suddenly, Aaron was overcome by a desire he had never felt before, complete with an erection so hard it was almost painful—extending his cock to a size he had never thought possible.

He positioned me on my stomach, my big round ass cheeks pointing skyward, and began to lubricate the hairy crack he found there. His lubed fingers probed past my sphincter and into my warm interior where they found my love button. I gasped with a mixture of tension and pleasure. Remembering what it was like for him the first time, Aaron was gentle and caressing. He stroked with well-lubed fingers as I started to relax and let desire overcome the fear of pain. He replaced fingers with his thumb and kept working, loosening me up even more. Sweat poured from me, and I groaned aloud at the pleasure coursing through my body. I lifted my ass and reached down to caress my cock, which was rock-hard and streaming precome.

"I'm ready, Aaron. Do it now. Do it now." I lifted my hips high and dropped my shoulders onto the bed to make it easier for the youth whose tender fingers had awakened such new levels of pleasure in my body. Aaron quickly slipped on a condom and, positioning himself, thrust his aching member, driving hard and fast, his care forgotten in the heat of desire.

"A-a-argh, a-a-ah, o-o-oh, mmm!" My scream of pain quickly turned to one of intense pleasure as my lover's rod slipped deep into my burning ass. I felt Aaron grasp my hips and pull me back, rocking my body onto his cock with an increasing tempo. My body responded lustfully, out of control. I bucked hard against Aaron's driving cock, and I could feel his balls banging against my ass with every stroke. Our passion built quickly, rising to a noisy crescendo that set the bed to banging and creaking, a symphony of sex sounds and smells that escaped the cubicle and had erections springing downstairs in the coffee lounge.

Simultaneously, we began to come. Aaron pulled free and ripped off his condom, jetting thick come across my back and into my hair. At the same time he reached forward, catching my cock head in his hands as I came with a blast that forced jism between his clinging fingers.

Afterward, we showered together, and as we dressed Aaron hesitatingly asked me to come back to his flat and stay the night.

"It's another first for me," he said with an almost shy smile. "I've always kept my fucks at a safe distance. I sort of feel someone in your own bed is more intimate. You're the first I've wanted there." All I could do was to grin my acceptance, as words just couldn't force their way past the happy haze of growing love that flowed all through me. Mr. Right, it seemed, had finally walked into my life.

That was four years ago and we're still great buddies, sharing a flat but no longer a bed. That side of our relationship ended a month or two ago without any nastiness. But what a four years. Lives changed, positively, forever, thanks to the passion and the chemistry that resulted in a chance meeting at a sex-on-site venue, all because of a canceled flight.

Champagne Surprise

Jeff Fisher

When in any bar, gay or straight, I love to watch people without their being aware of it. It's fun to try to figure out the stories of their lives and those of the people they are with. On this night, from across the smoky and noisy bar, I immediately noticed two guys who seemed to be arguing about something. Every few moments they would glance my way and then resume their disagreement. I did my best to not be blatantly obvious about my interest in what was happening.

The angrier of the two was blond and beefy. His massive biceps and bulging pecs stretched the fabric of his white T-shirt to the limits. The shirt was tucked into a pair of belted 501s that were worn thin in all the right places. A pair of old snakeskin cowboy boots finished off the tempting package.

The guy with him looked like the all-American boy next door. Incredibly handsome, he was on the verge of almost being pretty. His skin was smooth and tan and his teeth so white they seemed to glow in the dim light of the bar. He actually reminded me of some of my fraternity brothers with his clean-cut good looks. He looked a bit out of place in his button-down Polo dress shirt, khakis, and loafers. Looks can be deceiving, though, and I figured this fellow could have a real nasty streak. Little did I know I was going to find out personally.

The argument came to an abrupt end with the hunkier of the two shoving the "pretty boy" and stomping out of the establishment. The other guy took a deep breath and headed across the room directly to me. He stuck out a hand as he approached and said, "Hi, I'm Tim. Can I buy you a drink?"

I was somewhat stunned but answered, "Sure, a gin and tonic."

He was back in a few minutes with our drinks, and after a couple of awkward moments, I asked him what the big argument with his friend had been about.

"Oh, he's not a friend. That little performance was my lover at his best. He gets that way whenever we go out to a bar. And that particular fight was about you."

I almost choked on my drink. "Excuse me? What do I have to do with an argument between you and your lover?"

"Well, when we came in I noticed you and made some comment about your being an attractive guy. Scott got all bent out of shape. When he left he told me to go after you if I wanted you that bad. I told him I intended to do just that."

Still amazed, I listened to Tim as he explained all about his less-than-ideal relationship with Scott. After lots of stories and a couple more drinks, I was beginning to feel like a counselor instead of someone this guy wanted to pounce on. A half hour later Tim suggested we go somewhere else, and I agreed. I thought a change of scenery would do us both good.

In the parking lot we agreed to just take one car, and I got into Tim's BMW. His hands were immediately in my crotch, kneading my balls and shaft. He struggled to unzip my pants, and his face dove into my white briefs. My stiff prick was getting a good soaking through the fabric when Tim yanked my cock out of the fly and took the entire eight inches into his throat. All I could do was hang onto the dashboard for dear life as his mouth worked my meat.

I was about to blow a load when Tim came up for air and suggested we go to my place. I didn't even bother putting my cock back in my pants as I gave him directions to my house, just a few blocks away. We pulled into the driveway and up to the side kitchen door. With my hard prick still sticking out of my fly, I got out of the car, fumbled with my keys, and got us quickly into the house.

Tim fell to his knees and was again slurping on my cock. I lifted him up by the shoulders and kissed him. He broke away long enough to ask if there was anything to drink in the place. I told him I always kept a couple bottles of champagne in the fridge for special occasions. This certainly fell under that classification for me.

I kicked off my shoes and stepped out of my pants. Here I was entertaining someone I didn't know in my kitchen wearing nothing more than briefs and a T-shirt. As I got a couple of glasses from the cupboard, I could hear Tim shuffling out of his clothes. I turned around to a beautiful sight. He was bending over to pull his boxers off over his feet, and the most gorgeous ass was staring right at me. The perfect bubble butt was brilliant white, in contrast to his tan elsewhere, and totally hairless. His pink pucker looked very inviting. He turned around and presented the flip side of a body that defined swimmer's build. Jutting out from a trimmed bush was a long, thick, dripping hunk of meat that was getting harder by the minute.

I handed Tim a glass of champagne and dropped to my knees to catch the glistening drop of nectar ready to fall from the head of his cock, teasing the piss slit with my tongue. I stopped to fill my mouth with champagne and, without spilling a drop, was able to take half his shaft into my mouth. I swished the champagne around his cock and could feel the bubbles explode. I gagged and started to giggle as champagne almost shot out my nostrils.

Both laughing, we moved to the couch in the living room. Between drinks of champagne, we kissed, sucked, and licked every body part possible. Before long, the first bottle of champagne was empty, so I excused myself long enough to retrieve the other from the kitchen. The cork ricocheted off the wall as I opened the bottle. Tim was standing in the doorway as I headed back to the living room. He grabbed my stiff prick and led me down the hall to my bedroom. We again filled our glasses and settled on the bed.

Tim took my glass, set it on the nightstand, and rolled me onto my stomach. He took a big gulp of his drink and lowered his face to the crack of my ass. His wet lips gently kissed the lips of my asshole. He formed a trough with his tongue, and as it entered my asshole I could feel the cold, bubbling champagne flow into my hole. Tim licked, gnawed, and chewed at my ass ring. Every so often his tongue would flutter around the ring of my ass. Then he would plunge it inside me and suck the combination of champagne and natural juices from me.

He lifted my torso up off the bed into a classic doggy-style position. I expected him to begin fucking my brains out, but instead he started some serious ass play, first with one finger, then up to having four fingers massaging my insides. The emptiness I felt when he removed his fingers turned to surprise when I felt the cold glass rim of the champagne bottle against my ass lips. Still half full of champagne, Tim slowly and gently worked more and more of the bottle into my rectum. Then he would pull it out until the rings at the neck of the bottle popped out of my ass. In a fast movement he would shove the bottle back into me.

He then began faster in-and-out movements. Each time the bottle entered my body, I could feel more champagne pour into me. The movement of the bottle, and my shoving my ass back to meet it, caused the liquid to bubble more and more. I could feel foam running out of my ass to drip off my balls. Tim removed the bottle, and again I could feel his hot tongue licking the foam from my balls, ass crack, and hole.

I was repositioned on my back as Tim straddled my body so that his throbbing cock dangled above my lips. I opened wide to take in as much of the meat as I could. The bottle reentered my asshole as Tim took my man meat into his mouth. He was pistoning his own cock in and out of my mouth in sync with the bottle neck as it moved in and out of my ass. I felt lost in a fog of sex and man smells.

My ass felt like it was going to explode as the champagne gases expanded within me. Tim, sensing my struggle to not shoot champagne from my ass, pulled his meat from my mouth and got into position to plug my hole with his manly cork.

We were covered with sweat and champagne. I grabbed the head-board with both hands as Tim's body slid into contact with mine. I could feel the head of his cock as it pressed slowly into me. Then, with one sharp jab, Tim shoved his entire shaft into me, and I let out a scream. He began to fuck me like a madman. Both of his hands were around my cock, pounding me to the beat of his fucking.

We were both close to blasting our juices. I could see and feel every muscle in his body begin to tense up. The liquid in my ass was sloshing around as he entered me harder and faster. I saw white light as a stream of white-hot come erupted from my cock, adding to the sweat and champagne covering both of us. He began to grunt as he lost his load in me. Together, our contractions caused a shower of warm, bubbly champagne to spray out of my ass, around the plug of prick still lodged within me. We both collapsed exhausted. We woke later to a sticky, sweaty mess. That was OK, though, because getting clean was almost as much fun as getting dirty.

Friendly Couple

Donovan Lee

I should have known the night would start getting interesting when I uncharacteristically decided to visit the local gay bar during the week. There was only a small crowd (if I can refer to ten or 15 people as a crowd), but I managed to amuse myself with the intensified attention from the few guys who were there. Although I found their interest flattering, I didn't find any of them interesting—except for Al.

It surprised me when Al kept checking me out at the urinal; he's one of the cutest Hispanic guys I've ever. Even more surprising was that Al's longtime lover, Tom, was combing his hair in the mirror behind us while Al played with himself and smiled at me. How could I not look at Al's hard, uncut cock when he was standing right beside me jerking on it?

I looked, but I didn't touch that dark piece of meat. Instead, I put my own cock away and walked out of the bathroom. They soon left the bar, and I regretted not acting on the intriguing situation. I could at least have jacked off a little or returned Al's smile.

That Friday night, it happened again, with the exact same setup: Tom combing his hair, Al jerking his hard cock, me standing at the urinal looking confused. This time, I said hi to Al and glanced down approvingly at his hard stick as I zipped up my pants and walked over to the mirrors. When I said hi to Tom, he asked me to go dance with him.

Tom, a white guy with short brown hair, wasn't anywhere near as cute as Al, but they were both in their early 20s and in good shape. On the dance floor Tom kept rubbing his body against mine, occasionally making his crotch or his butt touch my hands. I got a good feel of his cock one time and could tell that it was quite big, so I decided to keep returning my hands to that special place. This night there was a real crowd at the bar, and much of that crowd was staring at our sexual display.

Later, Al bought us a round of drinks. We gulped those down between awkward glances at each other before hitting the dance floor as a trio. After a few more songs and a lot of "accidental" brushes against each other's boxes, we walked together toward the exit.

"Should we just take our car?" Al asked.

"I guess so," I replied, assuming he meant we were going to their place. I thought things might have been headed in this direction, but it surprised me to hear it stated so matter-of-factly.

He apparently noticed my look of surprise because he then asked, "Tom did invite you over for a three-way, didn't he?"

"Well, no," I replied, "but I figured as much."

Tom blushed slightly, then told Al, "I thought you were going to ask him."

"You both got the idea across very well," I said, smiling. After agreeing to leave my car there until morning, I got into their backseat. We mostly kept quiet during the drive home, occasionally touching each other here and there or just commenting on the dance tape they were playing.

After we all walked into their bedroom, Al told Tom and me to go ahead and get started, adding that he'd join us after taking a shower. When Tom got undressed I saw that he had something to compensate for his plainer looks, namely a fat cock of at least eight inches. After kissing and fondling him for a few minutes, I had him lie on his back with his legs open and that big organ sticking up.

I got on my hands and knees between Tom's well-toned legs, licking his balls, taking turns between those two impressive orbs. He probably needed a shower too, after all of that dirty dancing, but I didn't mind the smell of his sweat against my face. I also didn't mind making him sweat even more.

Eventually, I started running my tongue up his huge cock, teasingly approaching the head before returning to his balls, then going back toward the head. As I finally took the sweet-tasting dick head into my mouth, I felt Al's tongue enter my ass.

Despite how good that felt, it caught me off-guard because I didn't hear Al come in from the shower. I retreated for just a second from pleasuring Tom—but only for a second. Soon I was both giving and receiving some great oral pleasure. I took in as much of Tom's fat meat as I could without gagging while Al invaded me with his skillful tongue.

After a while in that position, we all lay down side by side and felt each other's bodies. Although it was nothing like Tom's monster cock, Al's uncut organ certainly wasn't a disappointment. He also told me that he liked my dick and soon demonstrated just how much he liked it. While continuing to feel Tom's cock, Al took mine into his mouth, accepting the full 7½ inches. Backing up a little, he let it fall out of his mouth so that he could bury his face in my pubic hair. While Al kissed all around my balls and the root of my cock, Tom and I French-kissed and rubbed each other's chests. Tom's chest was the hairiest of the three of us, and I enjoyed running my fingers through his hair.

Al slowly kissed his way back up to the tip of my cock and sucked it into his mouth. My hand reached down to his short black hair, which I caressed gently. But he didn't need any guidance to go down on me. He took every inch of my throbbing cock, again and again, going up and down like some sort of perfectly aligned pleasure machine. My increasingly loud moaning must have alerted him to the fact that I would've come soon because he abruptly stopped and stood up beside the bed.

"So who wants to get fucked?" he asked.

Tom quickly volunteered, and I added, "I want to suck Tom off while you fuck him."

"Sounds good to me," they both said.

After Al put on a condom and some K-Y, Tom stood on his knees on the bed. Al stood behind him and shoved his cock in with familiar ease. But that familiarity didn't stop Tom from moaning with pleasure. I lay down on my stomach so that I could lick Tom's monster organ while feeling up the bodies of both my gracious hosts.

Al's butt was smooth and firm in my hands, sliding back and forth as he worked Tom's ass. My tongue slid across the moist slit of the dick that had begun bouncing around from all that back-door activity. Al's pushing soon forced much of Tom's cock into my mouth, not that I objected. The in-and-out motion of their energetic fucking made my job easier and hotter.

"Yeah, fuck me," Tom would say, then, "Yeah, suck me." He was breathing so fast that I was afraid our fuck-and-suck session would only last a few more seconds, but it went on for quite a while. I ran my hands up Al's back and around to Tom's hairy chest. They seemed almost like one person but with twice the intensity.

In unison, they both said, "I'm gonna come." I pushed away in time to let Tom shoot off all over my back, drenching me with his hot come while Al shot inside him. They both moaned like crazy.

Tom disappeared into the bathroom again and came back a few seconds later with a towel. After wiping the sweat and come off my back, they flipped me over and went down together on me, taking turns on my cock and my balls. I jacked myself off the rest of the way while they caressed my body.

I woke up between them in the morning. Taking advantage of the fact that we were still naked, I decided on breakfast in bed. First, I went down on Al, licking and sucking like I'd never get another chance to suck him off. Of course, I knew that was the case, so I made the most of it. I told him to push me away when he was about to come, then I went back to work on his morning erection, sucking hard and fast. In just a few moments he was pushing me away and shooting jism all over his stomach.

Tom had pushed the covers from his own erection and was obviously ready for the same treatment. I didn't let him down. Just after finishing Al, I accepted Tom's fat prick into my hungry mouth again, sucking in as much of it as I could without choking. Soon he lifted me away by the forehead and shot all over the place.

We went back to sleep for a couple of hours, then they drove me back to the bar. Although it was far too early for any of the employees to be there, I noticed there were a couple of other cars parked near mine. I wondered if maybe the drivers of those cars had left them there to spend a night of passion with a strange man or two before going back to their cars and back to their lives. I wondered if anyone's night had been as good as the one I'd spent with my friendly couple.

Jason Di Giulio

I was attending the final phase of Officer Candidate School, summer, 1994. The Combined Military Academies of all of the New England states had sent us, their future officers, to an expansive training ground on Cape Cod to complete our transition from sergeants to lieutenants in the U.S. Army. I was between the junior and senior years of college, had a boyfriend at school, and was out to most of my friends. I had enlisted in the reserves back in 1991 to pay for school. Becoming an officer seemed like the natural course of action if the "Be All You Can Be" ads were true. I was moving up in rank, not telling, and they weren't asking.

Officer training was rough. We woke to physical training (affectionately called PT) every morning before the sun rose.

Following that, the day was filled with classes on leadership and tactical principles. Often there were practical exercises as well, all preparing the Army's future leaders for commissioning as officers. For the officer candidates of the Combined Military Academies, on the dunes and scrub brush of Cape Cod in the steamy summer of 1994, this was it. In 15 days, if all went well, we would be appointed to the rank of second lieutenant.

The platoon I joined upon arrival was a small one, having only 20 officer candidates remaining in it. OCS has a remarkable attrition rate, and we were down nearly 60% since the start of the program several months before. The people standing in the rigid ranks of the company formation were a tired and hopeful lot. I recognized some of the faces: a few guys from Rhode Island, one Connecticut guy with huge, endearing ears, and Jake Macomber.

Macomber was in the back row of the second platoon formation, and I filed into the open spot to his right. I snapped to attention and looked at him from the corner of my eye. I could see him hold back a grin, the taut corners of his mouth pursing with the effort. He leaned toward me slightly and whispered, "Good to see you, Dog." He was the one who started calling me that last year after deciding that my name was too long to say.

After the mandatory safety briefing, given by a wound-too-tightly lieutenant from Vermont, we were broken into small groups. I was partnered with Macomber. We went through days of classes, joking and smoking, waiting for the final training event—the leadership challenge course. This course was nothing more complicated than a series of mock battles set against Cape Cod's moist dreariness. We would be out in the bush for five days, during which we would act in various leadership roles while conducting defensive and offensive operations.

I had always thought that Jake was attractive. He had this manner about him that seemed to radiate sex, even in the dirtiest and sweatiest environments. His eyes were large and blue and set above well-defined cheekbones that sloped to a narrow chin. Jake's mouth was wide, almost too much so, until he smiled. Then his face would open into a toothy white grin. Jake's camouflage uniform hung from his wide shoulders, almost hiding his tapered physique under its bagginess. When he moved, hints of the body underneath could be seen. The cords in his legs, the bulk of his upper arms, and the plane of his abdomen all revealed themselves to the attentive admirer, which I tried to be as discreetly as possible.

I was thrilled, and at the same time terrified, when Jake asked me to be his "battle buddy." In the Army each soldier carries half a tent. When partnered with another the two halves would create a whole, thus giving the pair a place to sleep out of the weather. We set our "hooch" up near the back of the bivouac area, as close to the back corner of the campsite as possible. Jake explained that from back there we wouldn't have to hear anyone else snoring.

The days were filled with intensive exercises. Squad infantry maneuvers, movements-to-contact, ambush operations, and the whole gamut of the infantry field manual were our daily bread. Each night around 10 (2200 hours) we were released for sleeping. Jake and I climbed into our respective sleeping bags after stripping to our boxers, tired and sore from the day's events. He usually fell asleep quickly, but I couldn't. I lay there listening to him breathe, watching the light through the tent flap catch the narrow line of hair just starting to grow on his chest. For the first couple of nights, I was unable to sleep. I watched him, then my watch, and tried to dismiss the temptation to touch him.

Jake had never given me any reason to think he was gay or even curious. He never talked about a girlfriend or anything at home, but he was so gung ho about all our training that I never thought I would be able to do anything sexual with him. Sometimes I would catch him looking at me, especially after I had been looking at him, but he always laughed it off as a normal observation. Sometimes, though, there seemed to be a double meaning to what he said. The hopeful part of me remembered these moments, while the pragmatic side chalked it up to wishful thinking.

On day 13, while waiting for the evening meal to begin, he sat on a large piece of driftwood, stuffing dry dune grass into the holes in the camouflage cover of his Kevlar helmet. We were required to be "tactical" at all times, so disguising our personal equipment, including ourselves, was necessary.

I stood a few feet away, my M16 rifle slung over my shoulder. I was supposed to be keeping watch for any instructors while we took a break. We were near a small inlet, and the Atlantic Ocean sprayed a cool salt in the breeze. The wind was a welcome distraction to the hot summer stickiness of the last few days. Jake looked like he was making a grass skirt on top of his helmet. It looked like a bad lampshade.

"Isn't that supposed to be a little lower?" I asked him.

"It'll do."

"Looks funny."

"I wouldn't talk," he said pointing at me with a wide finger. "Your face paint looks like Tammy Faye with a hangover."

I laughed and pointed out that his cammo makeup was no better. The sweat from the day had worn most of it off of us.

"OK," he grinned as he pulled out a stick of green face paint. "You do me, and then I'll do you."

I nodded and tried not to laugh out loud. He handed the stick of paint to me when I walked over. I stood between his knees, a full head and shoulders above him. Jake looked up at me, squinting into the late-afternoon sunlight. I placed my left hand on his sweaty forehead and began tracing a tiger stripe pattern across his face with the dark end of the paint stick. Then I turned the stick over and filled in the blank spots with the lighter green paint on the other side. Jake closed his eyes and let out a soft, small mmm sound. "It feels nice, Dog," he said. "Nice and cool."

He reached up and wrapped his hand around my right wrist. His hands were much larger than mine, broad and tanned. He opened his eyes and looked directly into mine for a long, pregnant moment. He pulled me down to my knees, between his legs, and took the paint stick from me. Without breaking his gaze, Jake began to paint my face. His face was slightly higher than mine now, and I looked up at him. I could feel the cool stickiness of the paint stick moving on my cheeks and forehead. His hands were warm on my sweaty hairline. I just stared back, breathing a little too quickly.

Jake moved his face closer. He arched the paint from over my left eyebrow into a wide dark streak down the bridge of my nose and farther down over my lips and across my chin. His lips were not more than two fingers away from mine, and I felt the hot, tangy aroma of too much coffee and cigarettes on him. I closed my eyes and let him touch my skin, taking in his breath.

Too soon, he stood up and said, "There. Done."

Jake picked up his M16 and put his helmet on. He asked if I was ready and began walking back to the bivouac site. I took a deep breath and tried to force my heartbeat to return to normal. Tonight was a big night; we had a tactics exam.

I got the highest score in tactics and was appointed as platoon leader for the next day's patrols. It was to be the last day of the field exercise, and I was hoping to get to the rack and to sleep early on our last night in the bivouac. I circled the camp, met with my four squad leaders, and made sure there was a good security plan. I wanted 25% of the platoon on guard at all times.

Our instructors were notorious for their use of tear gas at night, and I wanted to make sure we had warning if they decided to pay us a visit. I knew it would be their last night to play with us, and I knew they had been given a lot more gas than they had used so far. After ensuring that the guys had food and water, I retired to my hooch and cleaned my boots and gear for the next day. After a dinner of tepid soup, roasted mystery meat, and Kool-Aid, I went to bed. Jake crawled into his sleeping bag about 20 minutes later.

Maybe I was worried about tomorrow's patrols. Maybe I was too tired to think about anything else. It was a sticky night, so I slept with my sleeping bag open, letting it loosely drape over me. I used my gas mask, in its green canvas case, as a pillow. I fell asleep almost immediately after Jake came into the hooch.

When I woke up, not too sure how much later, it was pitch black in the tent and stifling hot. The flap to the hooch was snapped tightly shut; this was the first night it had been closed all the way since we started sleeping in the field. I pressed the Indiglo button on my watch and saw that it was 2:30 in the morning. Outside, I could hear the bugs and the gentle crashing of small waves on the beach a few hundred meters away. I reached up and unsnapped one of the buttons on the peak of the tent. I opened a one-inch space between the two shelter halves and let the moonlight invade the darkness of the tent. With that tiny, desperate illumination, I saw Jake on his side, his back turned to me, his ribs expanding and contracting. He, like me, wore olive-drab Army-issued boxer shorts. The top of his, near the cleft above his ass, was dark with sweat. I shook my head and rolled onto my side, away from him.

A few minutes later, while I was going through a mental checklist of reaction-to-ambush procedures in my mind, I heard Jake roll over and felt the hot wind of his breath on the back of my neck. I had slept beside men in the Army before, and I went through basic training and infantry school without breaking the no-sex code. I wasn't about to start anything now. I ignored my growing erection and tried to pretend that the pungent smell of Jake's sweat didn't turn me on.

"Dog? You awake?" Jake whispered, his lips close to my ear.

"Yeah."

"What are you doing?"

"Sleeping."

"It sounds like you're awake to me," Jake said in a coarse whisper and nudged my shoulder with his forearm.

"OK. Trying to sleep," I answered.

He moved his hand under his head, up on one elbow. I could see Jake looking down at me in my peripheral vision. I rolled onto my back. He was on his side, facing me.

"I've seen you look at me, Dog."

I was glad it was semidark. The light from the unsnapped section of the tent roof might not show me blushing.

"Yeah? I look at everybody."

Jake grinned, his teeth large and white. The tent seemed brighter. He brushed the soft line of hair from his chest to his navel, slowly.

"Naw. I've seen you look," he said, rubbing his abs. "I've seen how you look at me."

I shrugged. "Whatever, man. I gotta sleep." I started to roll back onto my side, away from him. Jake put his hand on my shoulder as I rolled and pushed me back onto my back. He left his hand there.

"We graduate in a couple days," he said as he leaned forward. "I probably won't ever see you again."

I looked up and didn't answer. His hand on my shoulder was warm. He leaned forward, moved his face directly above mine, and pressed his lips firmly against mine. I opened my mouth and let his thick tongue in. There was a hint of old cigarettes there, and I moved my tongue around his mouth, almost as if I was looking for the source. I reached around him and ran my fingers through the moist stubble of his shaved head as we kissed. Jake moved his hand from his abs to mine and rubbed up toward my pecs.

Without coming up for air, we moved our bodies together. I wrapped my arms around his slender waist and traced small circles over the heavy muscles of his back, moving my hands up and over his shoulders. There were small knots of muscles that undulated there as he crawled his hand up to my left nipple. I stifled a small sound in the back of my throat as he squeezed and twisted it.

He pulled his tongue out of my mouth and smiled again. I grinned, taking a deep breath. I let my hands slide down the front of him, feeling the deep etches of muscles built by too many push-ups. When I reached the front rim of his boxers, he arched his back stiffly, grinding his erect cock into the side of my thigh. He moved against me, working his erection toward, and out of, the flap in the front of his boxers. His cock was narrow and long with a pronounced round head. A gleam of precome glistened on the tip of his dick and almost twinkled in the narrow light of the tent's open snap.

He let go of my nipple and reached through the front of my boxers, wrapping his wide hand around my erection. He rubbed it up and down, moving his thumb through the moisture there, lubricating my cock head with my own precome. I reached down with both of my hands and slid his boxers over his ass, and down his thighs. He angled upward and pulled his legs out of them one at a time.

Jake stopped jerking me off and moved my sleeping bag out of the way, spreading it out on the tent floor. He licked his hand and lubed my dick with his spit. I pulled him down to me and kissed him as he straddled my waist. He pulled my boxers and helped me slip them off with one hand. With them out of the way, he lowered himself onto me.

He broke the kiss and sat nearly upright, moving his hips in a slow circular motion. I could feel the aching head of my cock just barely poking into him, in that narrow place just inside the ass. He stopped, placed his hands on my pecs, and thumbed my nipples. I wrapped one hand around his narrow tool and rubbed the ridges of his abs with the other one. He threw his neck back for a moment, biting his bottom lip, and dropped his body onto mine.

I felt my cock push into him, the plushy interior of his ass contrasted with the tightness of him at the base of my dick. We rested for a minute, letting the feel of our connecting burn into each other. He leaned forward, and we kissed again. I sat halfway up, and Jake supported me by holding tightly to my shoulders. I clung to his waist, rubbing my fingers over the soft globes of his backside.

We began to rock softly. I moved in and out of him, slowly, savoring the stolen-moment quality of it all. I leaned my head forward as I pushed harder, faster, and Jake met each of my upward thrusts with a downward grind. He face contorted as he chewed his bottom lip, letting only small sighs escape from his mouth. After a few minutes of grinding, I started jerking him off while we fucked, watching his shoulders rise and fall with quickened breathing.

He came first, shooting thick strings of semen that covered my chest and ran in rivulets down my abdominal muscles. With his spasms and contractions, I came a few moments later, deep inside him. Jake lay down on my wet chest, breathing heavily. I felt myself inside him still, quiet. I rubbed his back while he lay there. Our sweat and his come made us slick, together.

When a few minutes had passed, and our heart rates had returned to normal, Jake rolled off me. He threw me a pair of boxers and began cleaning himself off with another pair. I wiped up and watched him slip on a clean pair of shorts and recline in his sleeping bag. I put on the pair I was holding, not caring if they were mine or not. He leaned over once more and kissed me sweetly, gently on the mouth.

"Thanks," he said.

I smiled.

He rolled over and moments later was asleep. I lay down in my sleeping bag. I couldn't believe what had just happened. Far off, down the wood line toward the beach, I heard the shouts and coughs of third platoon. Listening to the wheezing and sputtering sounds, I knew that the instructors had hit them with the gas, not us. I felt for the compact security of my protective mask in its canvas carrier and tried to commit every detail of this evening to memory.

A few days later, after passing our final tactical exercise, we were commissioned as lieutenants in the U.S. Army in a ceremony on the academy's parade field, where the instructors pinned our shiny new bars to our collars. I saw Jake, tall and proud, standing at attention while he was promoted, his face freshly shaved, the ruddy tan of the past 15 days making his eyes seem brighter, the corners of his mouth pursed to hold back a grin. I saw him wink at me when I was pinned. After, with the rush of parents and friends and congratulations, we drifted home in separate crowds.

When I polish my bars for duty, sometimes I think of Jake and where he might be. The corps of officers has never been the same for me since then. For the first time, I felt the esprit de corps, the bond of brotherhood stretch across that parade field in Massachusetts. For a moment, we were connected.

The Call

Shaun Levin

We've just had sex for the first time, and I'm on my back with the covers at my feet. His breathing is gentle and scared. When he swallows, his lips make the sound of a kitten lapping milk, of an old man sleeping, of a cunt being fingered. I feel the cold as come trickles down my side and onto the sheets. I wipe it off my stomach with the edge of the duvet and cover myself again.

"Let's go out for a drink," I say.

He laughs, and I can tell he likes getting fucked. It's a laugh that knows its place and likes to be there. He's mine, and I'll get more. I'll fuck him like that again, slower this time. What a surprise this has been, his coming into my life all of a sudden.

"So should we?" I say.

"Should we what?" he says.

"Go out for a drink," I say.

"OK," he says. "Where?"

Shit, where? Where do you take someone you want to keep fucking? What kind of places do people who like to be fucked go to? What if I get it wrong and he won't let me inside him again?

"We can walk along the beach," I say. "It's still warm down there at night. The air's soft and quiet. You can wear something light or something the wind will blow against your chest and the nipples I've been chewing on. Little stains of ink spreading on your silk shirt. I'll show you off like a trophy: 'Look, everybody, this is the gorgeous man I've been fucking.'"

"Fucking."

"Keep breathing like that," I say. "Play with your cock. And then we can stop for a beer. We can stop for a drink at one of the beachfront cafés. We can sit on those low chairs in the dark near the water so I can finger your asshole."

"And then?" he says.

"And then? Then we can fuck again."

Don't go. Keep my cock hard; keep making sounds of pleasure. Let me know how you love being looked after. All I need is your breathing to know you're there. To know you'll let me fuck you again.

"We'll go swimming," I say. "The water's thick and warm at night. I know a place we can strip naked. No one's ever there at this time of day. I'll fuck you in the water. You'll sit on my lap and I'll slide my cock into you. I'll lick saltwater off your back. You'd like that."

"Yes."

"Say it."

"Lick me," he says. "Lick me and fuck me."

I rub the head of my cock against the duvet till it burns. I need an ass to stick my cock into. I need to feel that engulfment when you press into a tight asshole, that grip that is like a homecoming. My balls are still hurting from the first time we fucked. I need to draw this one out, build up a second load.

"And then?" he says.

"Then I'll sink my teeth into your back," I say. "I'll bite your armpits. I'll drink hairy salt-air smells from your armpits. I love the taste under your arms. Lift them. Lift them for me. Lift them so I can bury my mouth in the thick bush under your arms."

"I'm ticklish," he says.

"Don't play games with me," I say. "You're the one who told me to come in your mouth. You begged me to stick my fist up your ass while you came."

"Lick me more, then."

"Let's just fuck," I say.

"Not yet," he says. "Tell me more first."

"More what?" I say.

If I told you what I really wanted to do, would you go away? If I told you I wanted to be inside you...if I told you I wanted to rip you open and stick arms, feet, and head inside you. If I told you all that, would you still want me?

"Anything," he says. "You can do anything."

"I'll piss in your mouth," I say. "Is that what you want?"

"Yes," he says.

"I'm dripping hot wax into your asshole."

"Yes," he says. "Do anything."

"I could kill you," I say.

"How?" he says.

"Have you done this before?" I say.

"No," he says. "Have you?"

"Not like this," I say. "But I've fist-fucked a German, and I've tied up a man so I could slap his face with my cock."

"Talk to me some more," he says. "Please talk to me."

"I just want to fuck you," I say. "All I really want to do is fuck you."

He whimpers as if I've just picked him up in my arms. *Why do men trust so easily? Why, even when I'm scraping nails across their backs or making them drink my piss, do they think it is joy? Why do men fall to their knees when you tell them to?*

"You want it again, don't you?" I say.

"Can we still go out?"

"What?" I say. "What the fuck are you talking about?"

"Fuck me," he says in that cockteasing voice, begging to be slapped.

"Are you alone?" I say.

"Why?"

"Just tell me," I say. "Are you alone?"

"Why do you want to know?"

I'm losing him. How am I going to fuck him this time? Has he ever had a real cock up his ass? Can I tell him anything? If I showed him what it felt like to be blindfolded on hands and knees, never knowing where the next backhand's coming from, would he remember me then? Will that be my gift to him?

"Do you live with your parents?" I say.

"We could go to a beachfront café," he says.

"Have you got a finger up your ass?" I say.

"I want your cock up my ass," he says.

"Put your finger there first," I say. "Lick your finger and slide it up your ass. Where should I fuck you?"

Is he in bed, his mother and father in the living room? Are those television noises in the background? Is he bedridden with a wheelchair by his bed? Has he done his homework? Is it his whisper that makes him sound younger?

"Fuck me wherever you like," he says.

"Just keep fingering your ass," I say. "Keep fucking yourself."

That laugh again, a laugh that's been slapped since birth. A laugh that mistrusts tenderness and binds humiliation to a fat cock up his ass. And then he's quiet. It's up to me to fill these silences with questions. Every silence is a cunt, an asshole, waiting to be fucked. *Is this the point where I fuck him? Is this the time to call him a fucking cunt and make him suck out my asshole?*

"Come fuck me in the toilet," he says.

"In the toilet?" I say.

"Just fuck me," he says. "Please."

"Why?" I say. "Does someone need the phone?"

"Please fuck me now," he says.

"Where?"

"In the toilet," he says. "I want you to fuck me in the toilet."

"With your face in the bowl?" I say. "Is that what you want?

"Yes," he says. "Anything."

"Get inside," I say. "Get inside and get down on the fucking floor. It stinks in here. Come and piss all over the fucking floor. You knew where you were bringing me. Get your face down. Let's see you with your little asshole in the air like some fucking dog. Spread those ass cheeks. Spread them so I can spit into your fucking crack. Hold them like that. Hold them because I need to get your hole all wet and slimy."

"I'm holding my ass open," he says. "Look. My hole is open for you."

"Because you're going to get my spit now, fucker. Keep your ass open like that. Like a nice wet pussy. Keep it open. I know how good it's going to feel with my cock in there. Feel the spit land on your asshole."

I cough up a wad of phlegm up from the back of my throat and onto my stomach. I gather it up and rub it into my cock.

"Fuck," I say. "I am going to fuck you so hard."

"Please," he says. "Please fuck me."

"Your asshole is nice and slimy now," I say. "Can you feel that?"

"Yes."

"I'll rub my spit in. I'm going to keep it nice and soggy. One finger first, stirring the spit into your asshole. Feel that? Feel my fingers loosening up your pussy? It's so hot inside your pussy. Tell me how hot your pussy is."

"Fuck me, please," he says. "Put your cock inside me. Fuck me."

"You want it badly, don't you?" I say. "You need my fist in there to make you happy."

"Tell me to open my ass," he says. "Tell me to open my ass so you can fuck me."

"Open it," I say. "Keep your face down on the floor. Keep it there. Fuck, your hole is so wet and loose."

"It's in the air," he says. "My ass is in the air for you. Fuck me."

"I'm going to open you up like—"

"Yes," he says.

"Open you up like a—"

"Yes."

"I'm going to bury my cock in your hole," I say.

"Fuck me," he says. "I want to hear you fucking my ass."

"I'm fucking your ass," I say. "Fucking it and wetting it and opening it up with my fingers. I've got my cock and four fingers inside you. Fuck, you are so hot. Keep your face on that stinking floor. Keep your mouth open and lick up that come while I fuck you."

"Fuck me."

"I'm fucking you," I say. "My cock's inside you and I'm fucking the living shit out of you. I'm pushing your head against the floor and you're fucking loving it."

"Yes," he says. "Don't stop. Keep fucking me until you come inside me."

"I'm going to come inside you," I say. "I'll fill your pussy-ass with thick come."

"Fuck me."

"I'm fucking you," I say. "You ass is so loose and you love my cock inside you. Keep your pussy open for me."

"Yes."

"Open up."

"Yes."

"Yes."

"Yes."

"Yes."

"Ah."

"Ah. Jesus. Fuck."

"Hello?"

I hear droning in my ear as I catch my breath. I set the receiver down on the bedside table. The house is dark and the room's getting colder. I pull the covers up to my chin and close my eyes. I hear rainwater in the drainpipe outside my window. Inside there's a peaceful darkness, and the house is quiet.

He wouldn't tell me how he got my number. *Was it a coincidence, like he said? His dialing at random and my picking up at 2 A.M.? And what if someone had heard us? What if he knows who I am? Has he got my number on a piece of paper with him? Will he call me again?*

Sunday Morning

Wes Berlin

*H*is name was Joey, and he said he looked like a miniature version of a life-size Ken doll. We met on the hardcore chat line. He told me he was sitting on his couch naked, fingering his ass and feeling a little unsatisfied. He'd spent the night being fisted by his steady boyfriend. Still, it wasn't enough, and at 8:30 in the morning he needed further stimulation.

I thought about going over to take care of him. His offer was pretty irresistible. But I was lying in bed, just waking up, and, though feeling horny, would rather have had him come to me. He told me he normally didn't have to go out because he was pretty much passed around among his buddy's acquaintances. All very good-looking, he assured me.

I remarked on his Boston accent, and he said he went to college there. In fact, it was during his junior year, when he was 21, that he discovered his true sexuality. Up until then, he said, "I was screwing every girl that would let me."

Then he met a senior on the football team who lived on the same floor in the dorm; "six foot five and about 250 pounds," Joey described. One night Joey got back to the dorm, and the athlete was a little drunk. He simply came into Joey's room and raped him. "But I got into it pretty quick," he admitted. "His dick was ten inches long and big around as a Coke can." *Aren't they always?* I thought.

"Well, we started going at it about once a week," Joey continued. "I stopped seeing girls and just waited until he was in the mood."

After his pile driver graduated and got married, Joey met a guy in the Boston bar scene. "He was the first one who really opened me up," he said. With kid gloves, no doubt.

And right at that moment, that's what Joey needed: a good plowing with another man's balled hand. I told him I wanted to come over and take care of him, but I didn't want to get out of bed. "Gimme your number," I said, "and I'll call you later."

He gave me the number but then said, "What the heck. I can't wait. I'll come to you." A half hour later I opened the door. True to his description he was a pint-size Ken clone with a shock of bleached-blond hair. He was wearing big sunglasses and carrying a brown paper bag. We gave each other the once-over; he decided to stay, and I decided to let him.

I told him to get undressed so that I could take a look at this ass I'd heard so much about. He put down the bag and obliged. He stripped down to a jockstrap and socks, then put his chunky construction boots back on. He had a smooth gym-toned body with a very narrow tan line. His right nipple was pierced, and whatever he had in the jockstrap was straining to get out.

I turned him around and gave his ass a thorough inspection, moving the straps of his jock aside so that I could push a finger or two into the pretty pink hole. He felt nice and tight. "I thought you were already open," I kidded. Joey just laughed.

Inside the brown paper bag was a can of Crisco and some rubber gloves. I put one on and dipped my sheathed hand into the can for a generous lump of the cooking fat. He bent over, bracing himself against the table, and spread his legs appealingly apart. I wiped a wad of the grease up and down the generous crack, twisting my hand around to get all sides thoroughly lubed.

Two fingers, three fingers, four. "Slowly," he kept murmuring. I pulled out and loaded on some more grease and gingerly pushed all five fingertips into his increasingly receptive opening. I pushed up to the knuckles, twisted the palm parallel to his cheeks, and eased further in.

"Take it out. Put on some more grease," he whispered hoarsely.

I did so.

This time it was much easier, and I slipped in up to my wrist. He felt nice and warm, my hand held secure in the muscular pocket. I carefully gathered my fingers and moved in more deeply.

He began slowly pumping back and forth, and I reciprocated. I reached around and pinched his nipples with my free hand, then twisted myself around so that he could get access to my steel-hard cock. He took it into his mouth, his lips clamped around the head, but the position was awkward and he couldn't take it all.

His ass bud opened like an iris, and he moved back and forth with ease.

"Put more grease on," he said breathlessly. I pulled out to oblige and went back in. This time he squatted down up to my forearm with his swollen dick staring me in the face. As he raised and lowered himself on my arm, I started biting his nipples and he began loudly moaning and rocking back and forth. He began jerking his cock, and I jerked mine. Then he suddenly let out a gasp and announced he was coming. I let my load shoot all over his work boots. I didn't see or feel his load and asked him if he'd shot. "Yeah," he said. Where? He pointed at my chest and I felt the droplets with my fingers.

Then there was that awkward silence and uncertainty that follows a shared orgasm by two strangers. I pulled my hand out and reached for paper towels, first holding them up for him to take a couple of sheets. I complimented him on his terrific passage and he asked me how long I'd been hand balling.

While he dressed I tidied up. Just as he was about to go out the door, he put on his dark glasses. For a second I thought he wanted to give me a good-bye kiss. Instead, he smiled.

I closed the door.

The Challenge

Jeff Fisher

It wasn't until I was 27 years old that I was fucked in the ass by another man. I'd given and received blow jobs and done my share of jerking off with other guys, but I was totally naive and inexperienced about taking it up the ass. In fact, when I first started going to a local gay-porn theater, I actually thought the films of men getting pounded by other guys were created by trick photography. I just knew that cocks as big as those on the porn stars could not possibly fit into something as small and tight as an asshole.

I'll admit, the first time a hard, dripping cock broke into my ass it was the most painful thing I had ever experienced. But, just as the guy behind the cock kept telling me, within a couple of minutes the pain evaporated into the most pleasurable feeling of my life. Far from being the "sissy" activity we all have been taunted about, taking a big, throbbing, hot cock up the ass is an incredibly masculine experience. From the first time I was hooked, and I have certainly had my share of man meat in my hole.

I think most gay men, whether they will admit it or not, tend to be size queens on occasion—or even all the time. I had always been concerned about my own size until I started experimenting with men and never got any complaints. In fact, almost every man I ever had sex with came back for seconds—whether I wanted him to or not. It gave me a lot of confidence socially and sexually with other men.

I'd heard rumors about this guy Gary for quite a while. Guys from the gym had seen him in the locker room and shower. Some guys from the neighborhood gay bar had even gone home with him. Word got around that his cock was so big it was impossible to give him head. Most guys wouldn't even consider letting him try to fuck them because his monster cock could rip them in two. Most often, the men he went home with had to fuck Gary or just jerk him off. All the things I'd heard about Gary made him seem to be somewhat of a challenge. Just thinking about it made my butt hole wet.

Gary was about 6 foot 3 with black hair and eyes so dark they almost looked black too. His hair was medium length, but some of it always was falling down across his forehead. An actor, he tended to dress in his standard drag of faded jeans, a white T-shirt, and a black leather jacket.

On one typical Saturday night some friends and I went to our usual gay hangout. Standing alone at the bar was Gary, looking kind of like a big "lucky dog" trying to make people think he was a tough guy. He glanced across the room, raised his drink to me, and smiled. Little did Gary know that the friend I was standing with was telling me about having gone home with him at that precise moment. Tim went on and on about how big Gary's cock was and that the most amazing thing was it actually got as hard as steel. He commented on how most guys would pass out from that much blood leaving their brain to pump up another body part. It was then that I took Gary's cock as a personal challenge. I wanted that thing in my ass! I raised my glass to Gary and smiled back.

As the evening went on, my friends got bored with the bar and wanted to move on. I wanted to stay and take on my challenge, but I didn't want my friends to know I planned to hit on Gary. He watched as my friends and I left. I winked at him and walked out the door. When we got to the parking lot, everyone agreed to meet at another bar. Except me. I lied, saying I had an early-morning appointment and had better head home. As soon as my friends' cars left the parking lot, I headed back into the bar.

Gary was just walking out the door by himself. He looked surprised to see me coming back in and asked, "Oh, did you forget something?"

I explained I really didn't feel like going to another bar with my friends and wasn't quite ready to go home. He immediately asked me if I was ready to go to his house, which was just a few blocks away. Not being a fool, I quickly agreed. Within five minutes we were at his place. As soon as we were inside, he pushed me up against the wall and kissed me roughly. Without speaking, we began removing our clothes as he guided me to his bedroom. By the time we were standing by his bed, both of us were completely nude with our dicks pointing toward the sky.

I couldn't do anything but stare at his cock. The thing was *huge*! It had to be a good 11½ inches long and as big around as my wrist. The purple head looked like it was the size of a tennis ball. And it was *hard*! Most really big cocks I'd had the pleasure of enjoying never got totally hard. This was definitely going to be a challenge.

The next thing I knew, we were on the bed and Gary was deep-throating my eight-incher. I had both hands on his veiny pole jerking him off. I couldn't begin to get the thing in my mouth. (Have you ever tried to put a tennis ball in your mouth?) However, I did my best licking the thing and mouthing his balls. Both of his hands were massaging my ass. Every once in a while a finger would tease my asshole. We were a tangle of arms, legs, fingers, mouths, tongues, and cocks. This guy was incredible.

Gary came up for air. "You've got a great ass. I've noticed you down at the beach in your Speedo. I'd really like to fuck you."

He had to know how much I wanted him inside me, though I admit that the thought terrified me. I really didn't know if I could handle the thing. He must have recognized my hesitation because he began telling me how not many guys would allow him to fuck them because of their fear of being physically hurt. He told me most of them just weren't willing to take the time to truly relax and prepare themselves for an incredible experience. I think his "actor's voice" had a soothing and calming effect on me. I rolled onto my stomach, and Gary began giving me the most incredible massage I had ever experienced.

He spent a lot of time concentrating on the globes of my ass. I felt him bend down and begin kissing my butt. The kisses were followed by a tongue wetting my crack and circling my asshole. As his tongue entered my ass ring, a loud moan erupted from my lips. He withdrew his tongue and replaced it with a finger covered with a cold lubricant. The lube seemed to heat up as it was rubbed into my hole. As I got more relaxed I felt another finger enter me. It was followed by a third and then a fourth. It felt like he was massaging the inside of my ass. My own cock had never been this hard, but I felt so relaxed I didn't even make the effort to reach for it and found myself gently humping his bed.

Gary lay down beside me and rolled me over on my left side. Lifting my leg, he placed his throbbing meat along the crack of my ass. With one hand he kept rubbing my head, my face, my pecs, my abs, and my cock. With his other hand he grasped his cock, moving it back and forth across my puckering hole. Each time it moved across the opening, he pushed it gently into me a bit more.

He was licking the inside of my ear and whispering, "Take a deep breath; relax and enjoy," over and over as if it were a mantra. I felt like Jell-O in this man's power; I was the most relaxed I had ever been with another individual.

Suddenly, he pushed hard with his groin and I felt as if all the wind had been knocked out of my lungs. I tried to scream, but no sound came from my mouth. The entire time, his hands were roaming over my body and he was placing little kisses on my face, neck, and back. He began to slowly rock back and forth. With each rocking movement a little more of his flesh disappeared into my ass. The pain was gone. In its place was an intense warmth and feeling of joy. Tears were running down my face. But they weren't tears of pain or sadness. Gary turned my head and licked the saltiness from my cheeks.

I lost all sense of time and surroundings. By this time I could actually feel his wiry pubic hair between my butt cheeks. If this wasn't nirvana, I don't know what is. Gary somehow positioned our bodies so that I was now getting it up the ass while on all fours. Each thrust was followed by him pulling his cock back out until just the head remained in me. My breathing was in unison with the pounding I was getting from this man.

Concentrating on what was inside of me, I had paid no attention to my own rock-hard cock. And I didn't need to. The massaging of my prostate by the huge piece of meat inside me set my dick off without being touched by either one of us. Both of us were completely drenched in sweat, and Gary just kept up a steady pace of moving in and out. In a short time I came again. After I came a third time, Gary quickened his pace. With both hands on my shoulders, he plowed into me again and again. Finally, he let out a scream like that of an injured animal and I could actually feel spurt after spurt of hot liquid deep inside my ass.

Exhausted, we rolled back onto the bed with his semi-hard cock still inside me. The sun was shining through the blinds when I felt him slowly slide out of me. Having met the challenge, I drifted off to a dream-filled sleep.

When I awoke mid morning, Gary had left for work. Beside the bed was a note saying he hoped we could do it all again in the near future. I got dressed and walked out his door. As soon as I shut the locked door, I realized I had locked my keys inside. With my ass a bit sore, I slowly walked to a nearby coffee shop. Quite far from home, I had no choice but to call my friend Tim to come get me. When he walked into the coffee shop, I'm sure I was a sight. I was exhausted and hadn't even taken a shower before leaving Gary's house. Tim just looked at me, grinning, and said, "Caught ya!"

That evening I returned to Gary's to get my keys. I also got a repeat of the previous night. I was certainly up to the challenge and enjoyed every minute.

The Driver

A.J. Arweson

*M*ike and I are sitting on the terrace at La Paz. You know—the one with the great sunsets. I have one hand wrapped around a drink and the other on Mike's thigh. The warm breeze is blowing, the sun is setting, and we're feeling kind of mellow. I get to thinking about how we met. It was 1973. I was doing a lot of traveling on business back then, generally all first-class, but not that trip...

I'm tired. The flight is fucked up. The whole trip is fucked up. Flying late out of LAX. No upgrade. Stuck in coach. Middle seat. Change planes in Cleveland. Cleveland's snowed in. Really fucked up. We land at JFK after midnight, six hours late.

The organization is supposed to have a driver for me, but I suppose that's fucked up too. The plane is stalled on the runway, then at the gate. By the time I get off the plane, it's nearly 1 A.M., and I'm almost last among the angry tourists and worn-out businessmen. I don't expect the driver to be there.

But he is. After a very tough day, something definitely not fucked up.

You've got to understand. Definitely not fucked up.

The man is incredible. Six feet tall. Lean. Black hair combed back from his forehead. Green eyes. I'm sure he shaved this morning, professional obligation, but his beard has already grown back into a manly stubble. His black leather coat is open over a white T-shirt that shows off his nice chest and flat belly, and things look very nice indeed beneath the pressed low-slung khakis.

I think that this can't be real. After all the fuckups this has to be a mistake, but there's the neatly lettered sign, right there in his well-manicured hands. It reads MR. ARVVESON.

"Hi," I say. "I'm Jim Arvveson."

"Good evening, Mr. Arvveson," he responds. "I'm your driver. It's been a long wait. You must have had quite a day." He doesn't give me his name. He takes my carry-on, then helps me with my overcoat.

"Yes," I say as we start walking down the long concourse toward baggage claim and the street. "'Definitely situation normal, all fucked up'" all the way from Los Angeles to here. At least until now." I look over at him and smile. If I was hoping for a reaction, I don't get one. He's looking straight ahead, steering me through the crowd.

"Well, don't worry," the driver says. "You're in good hands now. I've been told to make you as comfortable as possible." After we walk a few more yards in silence, he looks over toward me and asks, "Any baggage?"

"No, I'm traveling light. We can head right to the Plaza Regent. It's on Central Park South."

"I know the hotel, sir."

The limo is a shiny black sedan, understated and corporate and very luxurious. I settle back in the soft leather seat. Things are looking up. There's not much traffic from JFK at this hour. We drive in silence. I'm happy just to rest back on the cushions and admire the splendid view of the city on a clear night—and to admire the driver's broad shoulders, the black hair curling down over his neck. When he glances at me in the rearview mirror, he catches my stare and smiles.

By the time we pull up to the light at Fifth, I've fallen into a doze. The driver's voice pulls me back to reality—at least it seemed at the time like reality. From then on things get—well, they get unusual.

"Sorry to disturb you, Mr. Arvveson. We're almost at the hotel." He is looking back at me in the mirror. "Is there anything else I can help you with, sir? Anything at all?"

I mumble "No thanks" but without conviction. There's plenty this man could help me with.

"This is my last assignment for the evening, sir," he continues. I'd be happy to take your luggage up to your room for you."

Kind of an unusual offer for a limo driver to make, but what the fuck; this guy is way too good-looking to say no to. I should say "No thanks" but instead, "Uh—sure, if you have the time," comes out of my mouth.

"My pleasure, sir. I'm happy to help. Just step into the lobby and check in. I'll arrange to take your bag to your room."

We pull up to the hotel. The Plaza Regent isn't widely known, but it's one of the finest hotels in New York, a place that takes care of its guests and respects their privacy. The doorman opens the passenger door. As I walk through the glass doors, I look back and see the driver talking with one of the bellhops.

It takes longer than it should for me to check in; something about the room. Back to normal for this trip, I guess. "Situation normal, all fucked up." I stop off in the hotel store to pick up a couple of things I forgot to pack. All told, it takes about 20 minutes or so for me to get up to the room. It's a very nice room on the 14th floor. Wet bar, sofa in the living area, king-size bed already turned down. The lights are off, and the only illumination comes through the windows, with their magnificent view of the park, which glistens white under a fresh coat of snow.

The driver is nowhere to be seen, but there's my suit, already hanging in the closet, with my bag open on the luggage rack. The driver must have come and gone. I feel more than a bit of regret.

But then I notice that the shower is running. Just as the water is turned off, I look toward the bathroom and out steps the driver, dripping wet. He stands there and dries off. His body is in shadow, backlit by the open bathroom door, but what I can see I like. Nice. Very nice. He wraps the white towel around his waist and walks over to the bed. I'm sure my jaw has dropped halfway down to my chest. His skin is a light olive, and it shines in the soft light. The black hair on his chest and belly is matted down with dampness from the shower. He is smiling.

"Hope you don't mind, sir. It's been a long day. I thought I'd better rinse off."

I'm speechless. This isn't really a situation that the Wharton School prepares you for.

"You look a little worried, sir. Nothing to be concerned about. Just make yourself comfortable. Why don't you take your clothes off and lie down," he says as he pulls the covers all the way back to the foot of the bed. "You must be pretty tired from the long day, aren't you, sir?"

What can I say? I pull off my tie and toss it on one of the easy chairs. The driver stands with his back to me, looking out the window while I strip down to my boxer shorts. The towel is draped low on his narrow hips, almost to the crack of his ass. A few black hairs curl in the small of his back, just above the white cloth.

I lie faceup on the bed, my head propped up on a couple of pillows.

He walks over to the bed and puts one knee up onto the mattress. "Why don't you roll over, sir, and let me give you a rubdown. And let me pull off those shorts. You don't mind, do you, sir?"

I roll over. He pulls my shorts off, then climbs onto the bed and straddles me. The bare flesh of his thighs presses against my sides. His hands are strong, and he finds all the tension spots. I'm a bit nervous and start asking questions. You know, "Where are you from?" "How long have you been in New York?" That sort of thing. The driver answers in monosyllables, and I get as far as "What's your name?"

He pulls up onto his knees and leans onto my shoulders with his hands. "No need to ask so many questions, sir," he whispers. His mouth is so close to my ear I can feel his breath. He reaches alongside the bed and pulls a white sock out of his boot. "Here, I think this will help," he says as he stuffs the sock into my mouth. The sock is damp. It tastes and smells of a day's worth of man sweat. That shuts me up. I sigh and put my head down on the pillow. "See, sir. I can take care of everything."

I watch as he picks a black bag off the floor and puts it on the nightstand. I hadn't noticed the black bag. He pulls out a length of fine rope and ties my hands over my head to the bedstead. He knows what he's doing. The knots are loose over my wrists but snug enough that I can't pull my hands free. He's still wearing the towel, and as he moves I feel his cock and balls flopping against my skin. His cock gets heavier as he works.

"Time to roll over onto your back, sir," he says. "Let's see how you're doing." I roll over and now I'm looking right at his chest.

Black hair curls around his nipples. His armpits are nested with damp black hair. Tasty looking. I groan behind the sock.

He slaps my cock with the back of his hand, watching with satisfaction as it swings back, arching onto my belly. "Very good, sir. You're doing just fine." He reaches into the bag again. Lots of stuff in that bag. I'm still worried. But it's the kind of worry that gets my cock so hard it aches. He pulls out a black dildo, cast from life, with balls at the end, thick veins, and a big cut head. The model must have been a big man who was having a great time. The dildo is formidable. I shake my head and silently plead.

"Sorry, sir, I'm afraid it is a bit big. But once you're used to it, it should feel just fine."

He's straddling my legs, and he's a big man. There's not much I can do, but still I struggle helplessly while he lubes up the dildo. He works slowly, stroking the dildo as though he could get it harder, bigger. He slides back a bit, sitting up as he does. He seems to be enjoying his work. His erection tents out the towel. Impressive. He slips the greased-up head of the dildo between my legs. I quiet down.

"That's better, sir," he says. "This will be more comfortable if you just relax." He pulls off his towel and lifts my legs over his shoulders. The dildo is pressed up against my tightly clenched ass. The fucking thing is big. I decide I really will be more comfortable if I just relax. He works the dildo up my ass, slowly, playing, first around the opening. Relaxing me. He doesn't fuck me with it, just slides it in, slowly and relentlessly. My ass hurts, though not as much as I thought it would. And I've never seen my cock so hard. The head arches all the way to my navel, filling it with a pool of precome.

At last the thing is in.

"There, sir. That should keep you for a while. If you can keep quiet, sir, I'll take out the gag." I nod, and he pulls the sock out of my mouth. I swallow and take a deep breath. He leans over and checks my wrists. They're fine. As he straightens back up he pauses to kiss me on the mouth. A hard, openmouthed kiss. His day-old beard grinds into my face. He probes with his tongue, then sits back up and stands alongside the bed. "If everything's all right, sir, I just have to make a call. I hadn't expected to be out so late. Will you be OK, sir?"

I nod yes, afraid that saying no will get the sock stuffed back in my mouth, but I don't really feel OK. My ass presses down on the dildo's big balls. Every time I move, it changes the angle of the thing up my ass. And every time I move, it hurts. "Um, excuse me," I say. "It kind of hurts."

He looks concerned and asks, "What hurts, sir?"

"The dildo."

He kneels at my side and lifts my ass up from the bed. With his free hand, he slides the dildo almost out, then back again, nesting it as far as he can up my ass. He eases my ass back on the bed, then straddles my belly, pressing the big-balled dildo farther up my ass and stroking my aching cock with his ass crack. I almost come.

"No, sir," he says, "the dildo doesn't hurt. *This* hurts." He slips his hands along my belly up to my chest. He digs his nails into my nipples. I start to scream, but he blocks the sound by clamping his mouth over mine. He triangulates my nipples with his nails and squeezes harder. He sits back up and, with his nails still digging into my tits, asks, "Now, sir, is everything all right?"

I nod yes. I've broken into a sweat. The driver smiles. He gets up and heads toward the phone that's on the desk in the living area. The desk is at the far corner of the room, and he takes his time. His white ass cheeks flex in the light streaming in from Central Park.

My body is shining with sweat. *Why is the room so warm?* I notice that the heat hasn't gone off since I walked into the room.

The driver must have turned it all the way up.

I lie on the crisp hotel sheets, my ass stuffed, my hard cock dripping precome. The driver stands with his side to me, facing the window. He dials and waits for an answer, then talks quietly. He's in no hurry. It's a perfectly ordinary call. But the man is naked and has another naked man tied up in bed not 20 feet from where he's standing.

And he has a hard-on that gradually goes down as he talks. Fucking frustrating. All I can do is watch. I squirm on the bed, trying to find the least painful position. I lift my ass off the bed. I roll my hips down. I lift my knees up to my belly. But every change only seems to make the big thing feel even bigger, to work it farther up my ass. Each time I move, I groan. Each time I groan, the driver looks over at me and smiles. All the while, the room seems to grow hotter. Sweat pores off me onto the sheets. It seems like the call is going to take forever, but finally he hangs up and walks over to the bed. His half-hard cock swings lazily from side to side.

He walks past the foot of the bed and into the bathroom. Cock view changes to ass view. *Fuck*, this man is good-looking. Through the open door, I hear the thick stream of piss hitting the water in the bowl. He pees for a long time. When he comes out he stands at the side of the bed. His half-hard cock droops just an inch or so from my face. I look at it and look up at him, begging with my eyes.

He smiles and leans down. His crotch smells of soap and sweat and man piss. He lifts up his heavy cock and teases me, keeping the thing just out of reach.

"You look like you want something," he says.

I nod.

"And what's that?" he asks. "What do you want?"

"Your cock, please. There's a drop of piss on your cock. I want to lick it off." He stands there, not moving. I whimper. I beg. "Please."

He scowls and says "Pig." He leans in closer. By straining against the rope, I can just barely reach his the tip of his cock with the tip of my tongue. I catch a golden drop before it falls onto my face.

He leans closer, propping his torso over me with one arm. His cock is dangling over my open, begging mouth, so close I can focus on each throbbing purple vein. The cock head is just out of reach. He contracts his scrotum and a final few drops escape into my mouth. I open my mouth so far that my jaw aches. Now I really want it. I want to feel his cock growing in my mouth.

He shifts his weight over me and drops his hips until his whole cock is in my mouth. He lays his belly into my face, as still as a statue, while as his cock grows until it fills my mouth and stretches to the back of my throat. Only when I gag does he pull back and start to fuck my face in earnest.

He groans. He pounds his cock into my face with his hips. I desperately want to touch him. The rope keeps my hands over my head, but I lift my ass off the bed and wrap my ankles around his waist. Dripping sweat streams onto me from his face and chest and belly. I slam my ass into the bed and fuck myself with the dildo.

Just as I think I can't hold out a minute longer, just as I feel his cock swelling to drop a load in my mouth, he pulls back. He slides his ass along the sweat pooled on my belly until his hairy ass crack rests on my cock.

When I shudder, about to come, he lifts himself up a bit and says, "Easy, sir. Easy. Only another minute, sir."

He reaches behind his ass and grabs my balls, using them as a handle to pull my cock up and lodge it in the pucker between his legs. And then he just sits down. He's already lubed up, and I slip in until my pubic bone is flush up against the firm cheeks of his ass.

I groan and arch my back, forcing myself as far up his ass as I can as I fill his ass with my come. His long torso is tense with excitement. His head is dropped back and his mouth wide open. He shoots. Long loads of come blast over my chest, my neck, onto my face, into my eyes, into my open mouth. I suck up as much as I can.

The driver collapses into the mess on my belly. He kisses my face and dives deep into my mouth with his tongue, reveling in his own taste.

After a few minutes he starts to lift himself off me. "No, wait," I say. "I want to stay inside you."

But he keeps right on pulling off until he's sitting up on his knees, astride my chest. He's still rock-hard. His cock arches until it grazes the hair on his belly. "It's all right, sir," he murmurs, almost whispering. "There's one more thing. Your sweet ass, sir."

He reaches back and pulls the dildo out of my ass. My ass lips grab the slick thing as long as possible and close behind it with a plop.

He shoves my thighs apart with his feet, then slides between my legs and lifts my ankles over his shoulders. His cock is lodged against my ass. "I'm kind of big, sir, but I think you must be ready," he says as he slides in. Maybe the dildo helped. I don't know. He feels enormous. He doesn't give me time to get into the pain.

"Just relax, sir. Let me drive us home." He pulls all the way out and rams back into me. "Like this." He has my ass lifted so far off the bed that I'm staring at my own cock. I'm still dripping old come, but I'm already hard again.

He bends over and kisses me, grinding his stubble into my face, then arches back and keeps on fucking me. He wraps his hand around my cock and starts pulling.

He's fucking me so hard and fast I have sheet burn on my back and my head is scrunched up against the headboard. He pincers my tits with his nails and digs in.

"I think it's time for you to come, sir. I want you to come, fucker! Now, fucker!" His head is thrown back. His chest and belly arch. He lays himself into me in one final thrust. "Now, ass-hole! Now!"

I do as I'm told.

This time it's my come that streams out over my face, my nose, my mouth, and his come that fills my ass.

He collapses onto my chest. It's a long time before his cock softens inside me and he pulls out and lies by my side.

Later, I take a shower, and the driver rubs me down with one of the Plaza Regent's big Turkish towels. After he showers himself he crawls into bed beside me. "Mind if I spend the night?" he asks.

Without waiting for my answer, he turns out the bedside light and curls up against me spoon-style. He turned the heat down a long time ago, so the room is cooling off. He pulls the covers up around our shoulders. He wraps his arms around my chest. My ass is nestled against his belly.

Just as we're falling asleep, I murmur, "You never told me your name."

He kisses my neck and whispers, "Mike. My name is Mike."

"Uh, Mike?" I ask. "Hope you don't mind—this has been really wonderful and all—but just what the fuck was this all about?"

He's almost asleep, but he throws his leg over mine and wraps his arms around me a little tighter. "No problem, sir. None at all. We can talk about it in the morning."

I snuggle my ass closer into his belly, hoping to get a little more action. But the driver is asleep. One more thing that can wait until the morning.

Underwear Night at Charlie's

Peter Paul Sweeney

*I*n the 1980s, Charlie's West in East Orange, N.J., held an amateur underwear contest every Sunday night. First prize was $100.

Two or three or four guys stripped to their underpants on the sunken dance floor, surrounded by men in lumberjack shirts. The room always stank of poppers.

"Take it off!" the audience shouted. "Take it off!"

Sometimes they did; sometimes they didn't.

Charlie's West was located near the New Jersey Parkway, Exit 148. To get to the place, you drove along deserted inner-city streets, under rusty train trestles, and past empty department stores. The entrance was at the rear of the building. I usually got stoned in the parking lot before I went in.

One particular underwear contest sticks out in my mind. I stubbed out my joint on the edge of the ashtray. Cigarette butts spilled onto the car floor. I slid the roach into the plastic wrapping of my Marlboro box. Marijuana smoke escaped into the night sky as I opened the car door. I pulled my coat around me and hurried to the entrance. Music from three surrounding clubs—straight and predominately black—filtered into the parking lot. I paid my admission, checked my coat, and bought some poppers.

"You want the new issue of *Blueboy*?" the Gothic coat-check chick asked.

"Maybe on the way out," I responded.

I grabbed a bottle of Heineken at the circular bar near the entrance and elbowed my way into the horde jammed around the dance floor.

It was the tail end of the underwear contest. Three semi-naked guys flailed about to Donna Summer's "Bad Girls," the soles of their feet black from the filthy wood floor. The DJ, Little John, peered down from his booth.

A fat transvestite, wearing a wedding dress, screeched at the contestants.

"Shake that booty!" she screamed. "Shake that booty!"

Laughter circled the room, bathed in a shower of lit pinpricks from the revolving disco ball. I was stoned out of my gourd.

A tall, skinny guy, whom I'd seen in the contest before, ground his hips at some salivating old queen.

The second contestant, with love handles and a bald spot, shimmied in plaid boxer shorts. He was well past his sell-by date for an underwear contest.

I picked out the third contestant, dancing between the other two. Stripped to his jockstrap, he was a young, swarthy guy, short, with unruly black hair, well-defined arms, and furry legs. He still carried some baby fat. A pink appendectomy scar, like an arrow, pointed to his white cotton athletic supporter. His dazed expression suggested an innocence at odds with his powerful basket and hairy ass. A tiny gold crucifix bounced on his smooth chest.

The jerk next to me in the crowd blew a whistle in time to the music.

"Do you mind?" I said.

"Get her," he sniffed.

I uncapped my bottle of poppers and took a whiff.

"Take it off!" I shouted at the young guy with the hairy ass.

As the song ended, the drag queen pulled the microphone cord behind her tattered wedding dress to the center of the dance floor.

"This is it, girls," she said. "What do I hear for contestant number one?" She held her microphone over the head of the first contestant.

Contestant number one rotated like he was wearing a Hula Hoop. A cheer went up at the far end of the dance floor, near the judges. *Friends of number one,* I thought.

"Not bad, not bad," the drag queen said. "Must be those hips, honey."

She dragged her cord over to the man in boxer shorts.

"Your heart OK, darling?" she said to the second contestant. He wiped sweat from his brow.

"Let's hear it for contestant number two!"

There was muted, polite applause.

"Love that plaid," she said, walking away.

She stood in front of the third contestant. She made the sign of the cross with her microphone and turned to the crowd.

"Put your hands together for contestant number three!"

The audience cheered so loudly it almost drowned out my own screaming.

"All right, all right already," she said.

Contestant number three shifted from one leg to the other, eyes down. In the dance floor mirror, behind him, I saw his buttocks clench and relax.

The applause faded.

Onstage, the three judges deliberated. The contestants wandered around the dance floor, picking up their discarded clothing.

I checked how much money I had in my wallet.

The drag queen shoved her way through the crowd to the edge of the stage. A judge handed her a slip of paper. She skipped back to the middle of the dance floor.

"And the winner is—drum roll please—the winner is contestant number three!"

The crowd cheered.

The other contestants shook the winner's hand and walked off the dance floor.

"Now, ladies, the fun begins," the drag queen announced. "Every week we auction off the winner's undergarment for charity. This week it's—"

She looked over at the judges.

"Who the hell is it this week?"

One of the judges, the club manager I think, leaned toward the microphone on the table in front of him.

"It's the gay church," he said.

The drag queen slithered over to the young winner, who glistened under a thin sheen of sweat. She snapped the elastic waistband of his jockstrap. He jumped a little.

"How much am I bid for this lovely athletic supporter?" she said.

"Five dollars," someone shouted.

"Ten dollars," I replied.

"Twelve dollars," a third person said.

There was a pause in the bidding.

"You can do better than that, ladies."

"Fifteen dollars," the first bidder said.

"Come on, girls, it's for the church," she said. "You want to go to heaven, don't you?"

"Fifty dollars," I said.

People turned to look at me.

"Fifty. Going once. Going twice. Sold to the horny fellow in the back row."

I stepped forward, my wallet in front of me. I handed her the cash.

"Would you like to eat it here," she said, gesturing toward the young guy's crotch, "or have it to go?"

"I'll take it off in back," I said.

We walked through the swinging doors beside the DJ's booth. The bright lights backstage blinded us.

"The floor's cold," he said.

"What's your name?" I asked.

"Tony."

I looked around the storage area. A large silver refrigerator hummed in the corner. Stacks of beer boxes leaned against the wall. We were alone.

"Over here," I said. He followed, his street clothes cradled in his arm.

We walked over to the beer boxes. He put his clothes on the floor.

I fished out my poppers and uncapped the bottle. Tony cupped his hand over mine as he took a hit. I sniffed and put the bottle back in my pocket.

Tony leaned back against the stack of beer boxes. His creamy skin almost vanished against the beige backdrop.

"All yours," he said, his eyes clouded with amyl nitrate.

He folded his arms across his chest, covering the tiny crucifix on its thin gold chain.

I reached over and slid my finger into the front of his jock-strap. The back of my index finger stroked a thin line of hair that descended from his belly button. I pulled out the strap and looked down on the thick patch of black hair.

I knelt before him and ran my fingers lightly between his legs.

"That tickles," he said.

His jockstrap swelled.

I ground my face into his crotch, inhaling the musty smell.

"Oh, my God," Tony moaned.

I slid my head below him and mouthed the outline of his balls through the porous cotton. Tony pressed down, moving his hips. I took each side of the jockstrap in my hands and pulled until it fell to his ankles. He lifted one foot, then another, and kicked it away.

I sat back on my haunches, each hand on one of his powerful thighs.

His semierect cock pointed straight out from a thick bush of black pubic hair. He was uncut. The head of his dick peeked out from its fleshy sheath. I fingered back his foreskin and flicked the tip of my tongue against his piss hole. I licked the curved, shiny head of his cock. Tony let out a long, slow groan.

I took him in my mouth and pushed my face against him, sup-pressing a gag. My lips brushed the black hair at the base of his dick. Tony put his hands on the back of my head and undulated, fucking me in the face. I tugged at his balls with one hand and tickled his asshole with the other. His fingers stroked the hairs on the back of my neck.

It didn't take long.

"I'm getting close,'" he said.

I took him out of my mouth and continued pulling with my spit-moistened hand.

"Really close, man."

I lifted my face and looked up into his brown eyes. The overhead fluorescent lighting glinted off his crucifix. I ran my tongue slowly along the bottom of his dick.

"This is it," he said.

He buckled. I closed my eyes, tightened my grip on his dick, and pumped like hell.

"Jesus Christ!" he said.

The first spurt must have shot clear over my head. But he jerked again, and I felt his come, moist and warm, hit me just below the right eye. I rubbed his dick against my face as he squirted. It oozed down my cheek, dangled off my chin, and dripped onto the floor.

The air around me smelled like bleach.

Tony gasped for breath.

Finally, he softened in my hand.

Still on my knees, I reached over and picked up the jockstrap off the pockmarked concrete floor.

"I believe this is mine."

I wiped off my face and stuffed it in my pocket.

Tony's head was bowed. He held his face in one hand.

"Thanks," I muttered. I lay a hand on his shoulder. He flinched but didn't answer me.

I walked back through the swinging doors. The dance floor was jammed with guys dancing to "It's Raining Men."

I collected my coat.

"I'll take that copy of *Blueboy* now," I said.

In the parking lot I started the car. Madonna came on the radio. I poked the flattened roach out of the wrapper of my Marlboro box. I lit it, turning my head sideways to avoid singeing my hair.

I took a deep drag, held it in, and leaned back against the headrest.

The Gold Cock Ring

B.B. Wills

*A*s I waited for the train to stop, I noticed him sitting alone next to the window looking bored. I stepped onto the train and quickly settled into a seat that provided me, with the exception of an empty seat directly in front of him, an unobstructed view of his face and upper chest. The silver oak cluster on his blue epaulet told he was not a fresh Air Force recruit. His short black hair was military sheared to the skull up the sides, just long enough to ensure that running my hands over it would definitely send shivers up and down his spine. Dark, deep-set piercing eyes and a heavy 5 o'clock shadow screamed Italian—and, I hoped, stallion. His noncommittal stare into my eyes definitely sent a message, but did it say, "Yeah, that's right. I want to fuck you" or, "Oh, yeah, I'd like to break you in half, faggot!" A touch of potential danger always did excite me.

Luckily, the distance between my boarding station and the next station happens to be the longest uninterrupted distance of the whole trip. It provided me enough time to size up this Italian stallion officer—which, as it so happened, was exactly what he was doing to me. His legs were spread wide open, making me wish I had sat next to him. As he rubbed the thick stubble on his face, I spotted the gold cock ring that his wife had placed on his left ring finger. He made sure I saw it not as a message that he was off-limits but, as I learned later, as a test to ensure that I would still be interested in a married man. I certainly would not be turned off by any man that looked like him, whether married or single, even if he was just looking for a quick blow job rather than a hot fuck session. Now the question was how we would make contact and complete the transaction.

As the train slowed to pull into my station, he rose to exit right behind me. Standing just about eye to eye with me at 5 foot 7, he was about 40 years old, relatively hairless on the chest, and sported short but thick fingers. As we exited the subway system, he positioned himself ahead of me, stopped, and turned to await my arrival. So I walked up to him with a smile on my face. He grinned seductively, held out his right hand, and said, "Hi, I'm Mike. I have some time on my hands and wondered if you were as interested as I am." Not accustomed to such forwardness, especially from such a manly figure in uniform, I was momentarily stunned. But I quickly recovered and told him I lived three minutes away. There was not much discussion as we walked to my front door and dropped our coats on the living-room couch.

He pulled me to his chest, wrapped his arms around me, and held me tight. Short, tight, and strong he definitely was. Shy he wasn't. I expected from him what so often happens with married men: Without much to say and barely removing their coats, they unzip their pants and want only a quick blow job before heading home to the wife and kids. Not Mike. His tongue quickly found its way between my lips and deep into my mouth. As he sucked my tongue into his hot, moist mouth, his hands ran down my back, gripped my ass cheeks, and began grinding my crotch into his. His teeth nibbled at my earlobes, and he began eating his way down my neck. He unbuttoned my shirt with military authority, slid it off my shoulders, and bent over to suck my left nipple. Still gripping my right ass cheek, he moved over to suck my right nipple and worked my left nipple between his thumb and index finger. Quite successful at getting both my nipples raised an inch off my chest, he knelt down in front of me and sucked the length of my cock through my slacks, kneading my ass cheeks with both hands. I worked hard not to go totally weak in the knees.

As he stood up he slowly worked his tongue up my chest and deposited it deep in my mouth again. He held the back of my head and masterfully turned it from side to side as he kissed me hungrily. He lowered himself onto the couch and slouched down so that his ass was just on the edge of the cushion and his legs were spread wide open. I lowered myself onto my knees between his legs and began kissing the inside of his thighs, working my way up toward the promised land. His cock hung down his left leg and I nibbled at it, concentrating on the engorged head that was easily visible as it strained against the tight fabric stretching over his thickly muscled thighs. He stood up and slowly unbuttoned his shirt, letting it fall to the floor, revealing a thickly muscled chest, stomach, shoulders, and arms. Surprisingly for an Italian, an almost hairless chest was capped by his large round nipples, which were surrounded with black hair. He unclasped his belt, unsnapped and unzipped his pants, then pushed them wide open. I reached up and gripped both his pants and boxers and pulled them down to his ankles, coming face-to-face with five soft inches of perfectly hooded Italian sausage. Framed by jet-black curly hair, his prick hung straight down about twice as far as his balls. All his body hair was obviously confined to the lower half of his body, as the dense crotch hair was only over-shadowed by the thick black hair on his legs.

I sucked his uncut dick deep into my mouth and worked its length with my tongue. I worked the tip of my tongue into the hood covering his bell-shaped head. He let me know that he enjoyed what I was doing as he held my head with both his hands. When he released his grip I slid his thickening cock out of my mouth and turned all my attention to his walnut-size balls. As I washed them gently with my tongue, his cock grew continuously, and I stroked it slowly with my hand. As blood continued to flow into his cock, it didn't get much longer, but it got thicker and thicker. I pulled back his foreskin, revealing the bell-shaped cap with the biggest piss slit I'd had the pleasure of seeing in a long time. I worked the tip of my tongue into that slot and licked up the glistening precome that shimmered there. He leaned forward and suggested we take it up to the bedroom to be more comfort-able. As he led the way up the stairs in front of me, I was mes-merized by his rock-hard ass with perfectly rounded cheeks.

I lay down on my back, and he straddled me, slowly inching his way up my body until his cock and balls hung down in front of my chin. I sucked his cock back into my mouth as I grasped his ball sac and pulled it down tight with my right hand. He grabbed some lube from the nightstand and reached back to finger-fuck my hot, hungry asshole. First the index finger, then two fingers, and final-ly three thick, strong fingers; my asshole screamed both from being stretched so wide and from wanting his cock so badly. I gripped his cock, dabbed a drop of lube on his dick head, rolled a condom onto his length, and lubed it up as he slid his way down, forcibly spreading my thighs wide open. He centered his weight on his knees, raised my calves up onto his shoulders, and pressed his prick into my hungry hole. Slowly, without hesitation, he masterfully filled me with his thick, throbbing prick till I felt his balls press against my ass. With a gaze fixed into my unblinking eyes, he let me know that he was going to fuck me until we shared the come that was boiling inside both of us.

With all the power that you hope for from any man, but expect from a married man who must keep the wife satisfied, he pumped the full length of his cock in and out of my ass, slapping his balls against me with each thrust. As time passed, his rhythm increased and our breathing became shallower and more labored. My eyes rolled back into my head as I reached up and clamped onto his nipples with both hands. His thrusting approached pounding intensity as my hungry asshole worked feverishly to grip his cock, milking it for all it was worth. Mike grasped my hard-on with his lubed hand and began stroking in perfect timing with his fucking. He sensed the pending explosion welling up from my come-filled balls and pounded his cock harder than ever into my ass. As my cock became more rigid than I thought possible, he withdrew from my asshole, ripped the condom off his dick, and quickly wrapped his hand around both our cocks. Stroking the full length of our perfectly matched cocks, he didn't stop until my chest was criss-crossed with alternating streams of our come.

As we stood at the front door, he kissed me as deeply as he had when we first entered the living room. Saying good-bye, he thanked me for a great evening and disappeared into the night. That was two years ago, and Mike continues to visit like that at least once a week.

The Handyman

Trevor J. Callahan Jr.

People always assumed that since I am a good-looking guy, interesting things must happen to me. And they're usually right. Since I moved to my new apartment about a month ago, however, I began to wonder if anything interesting would ever happen to me again. I couldn't believe this neighborhood! Jogging on a quiet leaf-strewn sidewalk, I felt like I was the only person in the world under 70. Who would have guessed that a college town could be full of nothing but blue-haired old ladies and elderly men with their pants up to their armpits?

Case in point: I had stopped jogging in front of my building to check my pulse rate. Panting lightly, I ran a hand through my short-cropped blond hair, then wiped the sweat on the white T-shirt I wore that hot July day. The well-manicured sidewalks were great for jogging, and the university gym was only two blocks away. But this was summer, so none of the students were around. Although grad school would start in just a couple of months, I had yet to meet anyone else in my program, or anyone in the department even. The only person I ever saw was my old lady landlord, and all she ever wondered was whether or not I could walk her enormous rottweiler, Fluffy. (I kid you not!)

"Trevor," I heard a voice quaver behind me. Speak of the devil.

"Yes, Mrs. Cavendish?" I said. She peered at me through her thick frosty glasses. Typical of her New England heritage, she gave me a small frown before continuing.

"The glazier called earlier. He said he would stop by late this afternoon." I had broken a window while moving in. "I told him you would be here. And the electrician is coming by tomorrow morning."

I groaned. Just what I wanted to do all day—wait for some handyman who probably wouldn't show up. "Sure thing, Mrs. Cavendish."

"Good." She turned to leave. "Oh, and can you walk Fluffy after the glazier leaves?" She left before I could answer.

This was my life. Interesting? Hardly. I walked up the stairs to the second floor and into my apartment. It was sparse but comfortable. The polished hardwood floors gleamed in the early-morning sunlight. "Nine o'clock," I said, looking at the clock. I had a 10 o'clock appointment at the financial aid office. I threw my jogging clothes into the hamper and turned on the water in the shower. I love taking showers; nothing is more relaxing. Stepping inside, I felt the water run slowly over my sweaty brow. Turning my face to the stream, I let the water dribble over me before shaking my head clear of the warm droplets.

I slowly began to soap my body. I must admit, I keep myself in good shape. My broad shoulders, smooth, muscular chest, and slim, firm waist were soon covered in lather. I bent to clean my athletic legs and wiped the soap quickly over my round ass before I began to lather my cock. This I did slowly, savoring the feeling of the warm water and the slick soap on my slowly stiffening prick. I let out a slight moan as my cock reached its full seven inches. I stroked it gently, my hand caressing the shaft, my eyes closed, and my head reclining on my shoulders, just enjoying the feeling of my fist on my cock, as if all the sensation in my body was now located in the seven throbbing inches I had in my hands.

A loud bang from outside startled me into letting go. My mood shattered, I quickly finished my shower and dried myself off with a towel. Stepping out of the shower, I brushed my teeth and combed my hair before loosely slipping on my fleecy white robe. Padding into my bedroom, I began rooting through my underwear drawer for my lucky black-and-white-checked boxers (I always need good luck when visiting financial aid) when I heard the second bang.

Looking out the window, I saw the head and shoulders of a man on a ladder. Surprised, I dropped my underwear and backed out of my bedroom into the living room. "What the hell?" I said, before realizing who that guy must have been—the glazier, here to fix the window. And Mrs. Cavendish said he'd be here this afternoon. *Old broad needs to turn up her hearing aid*, I thought. Then I suddenly realized I could feel a slight breeze on my cock and balls. Looking down, I noticed that in my surprise my robe had come open. Great. Not only had the glazier surprised me, but he'd also gotten a look at my still half-hard cock. Just great. And the guy. He was hot. I had only seen him for a split second, but I noticed piercing dark eyes, curly black hair (I love curly dark hair), and broad shoulders framing the window.

A knock at the door interrupted my thoughts. Shit. I knew who it was going to be. I was too embarrassed to answer the door, but the guy already knew I was home.

"Hi," he said when I came to the door. The rest of him was as good as the glimpse I had caught at the window. He was tall, with an athletic build, and a wide, easy smile that, at that particular moment, was fixed in a broad smirk on his face.

I felt my face turn red. "Hey," I mumbled, looking at his feet. The guy just kept smiling. "Can I use your bathroom?" he asked. I just nodded and pointed, watching as the guy headed for the john. His tight jeans displayed a nice firm ass. And the guy's bulge was huge. As I stood there waiting for him to come back from the bathroom, I couldn't help but imagine what that cock was like outside of those jeans. Just thinking about it gave a rise to my already-horny cock. Annoyed, I was pushing it back between my legs when I felt someone watching me. The guy was leaning against the living room wall, his smile still plastered on his face.

I quickly turned my back. "Uh, sorry about that display back there," I said, completely mortified, indicating the bedroom. "I didn't know you were gonna be there."

"Obviously," the guy said, amused. I figured that since he had used the bathroom he would leave, but he stayed right where he was. "But, hey," he finally said, "if I had a bod like yours, I'd be showing it off too."

"Yeah?" I said, pleased at the compliment. "Thanks. You look in pretty good shape yourself." *Damn good shape*, I was thinking.

"Thanks," the guy said. "I haven't seen you around. Just move in?

"Yeah," I said. "I'll be going to grad school over at the university in the fall."

The guy slowly crossed the room to face me. "I'm Neal," he said, extending a hand.

I eyed the outstretched hand for a moment, then finally removed one of my own from my lap, where I was still trying to conceal my semi-hard dick. "Trevor. Nice to meet you."

"Likewise." The guy was not returning my hand. Instead, he held it firmly in his own. "Since I've got this," he said, indicating my hand, "perhaps I can help you out with that." While he was saying this, he reached down with his free hand and grabbed my cock.

Instant hard-on.

My eyebrows shot up as Neal's rough, meaty hand wrapped around my shaft. "You know," Neal continued, "you look much better with this open." He pushed my robe open, off my shoulders, and onto the floor. "You do have a fabulous bod," he said huskily.

"Thanks," I gulped, a little nervous and damned turned on as I felt Neal's dark eyes boring into my own. With his hand still firmly on my cock, Neal began to kiss me. Our lips met, and I opened my mouth for Neal to explore. I felt Neal push his tongue deep into my mouth. His hands were now exploring my body all over, one meaty paw grabbing at my firm ass while another rubbed over my smooth chest. I felt my cock stabbing into Neal's denim-covered bulge. He began to grind his crotch into mine, and the rough denim rubbed roughly over my shaft. I found myself moaning as Neal bent his mouth toward my left nipple. He grabbed the nip with his teeth and twisted, causing me to moan even louder. Neal pushed me onto the couch and knelt before me, his lips still exploring my chest while his hands reached for my filling balls. Roughly, he squeezed my balls while his lips moved lower, down my abs and waist, toward the first stray pubic hairs before he finally buried his mouth and nose into my thick blond bush. I gasped as he squeezed my sac again, and in that instant Neal had lowered his mouth onto my hard, glistening cock.

I felt Neal's tongue on the head of my shaft and saw stars. He licked the head and slowly moved down the entire shaft, taking more and more of my cock until his nose was again buried in my pubes. He began to move his mouth up and down my shaft, sometimes sliding the cock out of his mouth to lick up and down the shaft, sometimes languorously licking the head, my piss slit leaking precome, and sometimes just bobbing his head up and down on my aching cock. My unchecked groaning told Neal that I was having a very good time.

This went on for several minutes; just when I thought I was going to blow my wad, Neal abruptly stopped and stood in front of me. I could see the hard outline of his tool in his denim jeans and began to slowly rub my hand over it. I moved my mouth to cover the thick tool and began to delicately gnaw on his growing cock. I felt his hand on the back of my head, pushing my mouth roughly on his denim-covered bulge. My eyes swam as Neal fucked my face through his jeans. Backing off for an instant, he finally released his cock. I was amazed at its size. It was perfectly formed, with a large head, thick, and at least eight inches of juicy-looking shaft. "Jesus," I muttered before Neal's hand directed my eager mouth back onto its prize. I took the bulbous head into my mouth and got my first taste of Neal's sweaty cock. I almost choked as he forced his cock farther and farther down my throat, but it felt so good to have my mouth filled with cock that I didn't care.

I sucked his cock for several minutes as Neal directed the action with one or both of his hands, his eyes closed in pleasure. At one point Neal stripped his shirt off, stepped out of his shoes, and kicked off his pants. Naked, he watched as his thick, strong cock disappeared again and again into my eager waiting mouth.

Eventually releasing my mouth from its service, Neal pulled me to a standing position and wrapped his arms around me. Kissing deeply, we slowly made our way back to the bedroom. I felt myself being pushed onto the bed. "On your stomach," he barked. "Put your ass in the air." I complied and was sweetly rewarded when Neal began to tongue my hole.

"Oh, my God," I said. "Yeah, man, that's it. Jesus—shit! That feels fucking awesome." And it did. Neal shoved his tongue again and again into my hungry pink ass. "Yeah, man," I said. "Fill that hole with your tongue."

Neal removed his tongue and began to probe my ass with his fingers. "Get me a condom, buddy, and I'll fill that hole with something else." I reached over to my nightstand and removed a rubber and some K-Y. "Put it on me," he said. Obediently, I turned around, opened the condom wrapper, and stretched the rubber over Neal's huge cock.

"Jesus, will it even fit?" I muttered as I slid on the condom.

"You bet it will," he said. I squeezed some K-Y onto the palm of my hand and greased up his cock. I had never felt a cock so rigid and hard before. "Assume the position," he said, and I eagerly obeyed, thrusting my hips and waiting ass into the air. After working some lube deep inside me, Neal removed his fingers and positioned the head of his cock at my hole. I could feel the power of his cock waiting to rip me open. "You want it, boy?" he said. "Let me hear you beg for it."

"C'mon, man," I said. "You know you wanna fuck my hole. Give me that hot cock. C'mon, man, don't tease me. I'm so hot for your cock, man. I'm dying for some cock. C'mon, fill me up with that huge prick. C'mon, man, I got a real tight hole. Fuck me, dude, c'mon—oh, shit!" I yelled as Neal's cock thrust forward and penetrated my hole. "Jesus fucking Christ!" I shouted in total pleasure as Neal began to plow my ass. I could feel Neal's heavy balls slapping against my own and hear the powerful *thwup thwup* of his thighs slapping against my backside.

"Oh, yeah, boy," Neal panted, "you sure do have a tight hole." He began to fuck me hard, slapping my ass as he fucked me, his breath coming in pants and beads of sweat dripping from his brow and onto my back. I was gritting my teeth and clutching at the bed. I had never been fucked this hard, but it felt great.

"Oh, yeah!" I said over and over.

Neal pulled out his whole cock and plunged it right back in. I thrashed in pleasure. He did it again and again, sometimes delaying entry to tease me, sometimes only going in halfway before pulling out. It was pure torture—my ass was on fire the whole time—and I was loving every minute of it.

Neal pulled his cock out of me and slapped me on the ass, indicating that I was to move. He lay flat on his back, his huge cock stretching toward the ceiling. "Climb aboard," he told me. Grinning, I straddled Neal's hips and slowly slid my ass down his pole.

"Oh, yeah," I said as the air was forced out of me by Neal's throbbing cock.

"Ride it, boy," he said, and I began to bob my ass up and down on his swollen prick. At the same time Neal began to buck his hips to meet my thrusts so that every time his cock was shoved up my ass, I thought it was going to come out of my throat. With his free hand, Neal grabbed my hard, dripping cock and began to jerk me off.

"Man, if you keep that up, I'm gonna shoot," I said.

"Do it," he commanded. Still bobbing up and down on his dick, I felt my leg muscles tense and convulse as my balls began to tighten firmly.

"I'm gonna shoot!" I shouted.

"Do it, boy! Shoot!" he said, jerking his hand even harder on my raw cock. Just then globs of sticky white come began to shoot from my cock all over his chest. Yeah, yeah, yeah! I shouted, still furiously riding Neal's cock.

My pulsing ass muscles pushed Neal's cock over the edge. "I'm gonna shoot up your ass, boy! I'm gonna blow in your hole!" he yelled, thrusting his cock up and into me.

"Do it, man!" I shouted. Neal squeezed his eyes shut, his whole face convulsing in pleasure.

"Here it comes, man, I—u-u-ugh!" he moaned as his load began to flow from his cock.

Panting, we stayed that way for several minutes, enjoying the exhaustion of the moment, his throbbing cock still firmly up my ass, before my twitching leg muscles gave in and I slid off of him, his thick prick sliding out of me in one warm, fluid motion. "Wow," I said after a minute. "That was hot." I nestled myself into the crook of Neal's arm and wiped my own load into his tanned skin. "I wish all the handymen around here were as hot as you. Tomorrow the electrician comes, and he's probably some fat pig."

Neal gave me a wolfish look and grin. "The electrician is my lover, Scott," he said. Noting my surprised look, he said, "Relax. We have an understanding about these things. And if you think I'm good in bed—" he left the thought unfinished.

"Damn," I said, absorbing it all. "For real? If that's the case, I'm gonna have to start breaking some more stuff around here."

Out of the Closet

William Holden

Johnny's was a small-town bar in the middle of a dull German neighborhood on the west end. It didn't matter; my heart raced with anticipation as I entered. At 24 and still a virgin, I was primed and needed release. The room was lit with only a single candle on each table, for a total of five. There was also a curiously seductive glow from the pink neon sign that spelled out the bar's name. I wanted desperately to turn around and run, but my body wouldn't let me. I stood paralyzed for what seemed like hours. Finally, I walked over to the bar and ordered a drink.

As I sat there I felt the most incredible sensation—as if the man sitting next to me was undressing me with his eyes.

Wanting to see more of him, I turned my head slightly. I met the most piercing brown eyes of my life. They were tearing into my clothes. His smile widened as he noticed my attention. His olive skin was flawless. Immediately, I yearned to touch it. He had beautiful shoulder-length midnight-black hair. I couldn't help wondering what it would be like to run my fingers through it as we fucked. To feel it sweaty against my face. My balls began to tighten. "Hi, my name is Doug," he said, reaching out to shake my hand. As our hands touched, the electricity ran through me.

"I'm Kevin," I said, my hand still in his. My mind pleaded with him not to let go. We sat there for a moment, looking at each other until I couldn't take it any longer. "Can I buy you drink?" I asked nervously. He continued looking at me and began tracing my forearm with his finger.

"Yes, on one condition: you spend the night with me." A seductive smile swept over his face as if he knew my answer even before I did. I was sexually charged. I was also terrified of what I was getting myself into. My heart was doing triple-time, and my entire body started to tremble. I looked into his eyes and swore I could see paradise. At that moment I knew what I had to do.

"Then what will you have?"

"A screwdriver," he smiled.

I ordered us two. Neither of us spoke a word.

"That'll be $5.75." The bartender broke our silence. I reached into my pants to bring out the money. As I did, Doug's eyes followed every move of my hand, watching every curve, every movement inside my pants. My cock began to harden as I reached in deeper for the cash. As I turned back, his face was inches from mine. He kissed me gently. I could taste the alcohol fresh on his lips. The minute he pulled away, I knew I wanted more.

I wanted more of his lips, more of his smell. I needed it. I slowly lifted my hand to his face. His jawline was square and already rough with the start of his morning beard. I dropped my hand to the back of his neck and pulled him closer. He looked surprised at my advance yet immediately excited. We kissed again. I let my lips linger on his. As I pulled away he brought his teeth down on my lower lip as if to stop me. Then he let go and sank his mouth onto mine. His tongue began to move inside me, caressing and tasting every corner of my mouth. His breath was hot on my face as we leaned our foreheads together. His hand began exploring the curves and roadways of my legs to find the shortest route to my sex tool. He did.

As he traced the outline of my enlarged cock, I could feel my wetness beginning to drip. The first signs of precome began trickling down my enlarged member.

"So when can I have your phone number?" he asked, still tracing my crotch. "I don't think we can go much longer in this place without being thrown out."

"Why don't you just come back with me?" I asked. "We're only a few minutes from my place."

"I'd rather take you home with me," he replied, still circling the outline of my cock with his finger. "I just need to go home first to make sure everything is perfect for your arrival." His smile widened, and for the first time I was sure of how much he wanted me.

"Do you have a pen?" he asked. The bartender broke in to hand him a large felt-tipped black marker. "A little large for writing with," I noted.

"Not when you have something large to write on." He slowly began to unbutton his shirt, his eyes never leaving mine. My cock pulsed with each new button he released. His chest was smooth, not a trace of hair anywhere. As he opened more of his shirt, the dark rounds of his nipples appeared. I yearned to touch them, to lick them. I followed his every move until his shirt was opened to his navel. "Write your number here," he said, pointing to the space between his nipples. "That way I won't lose it."

I took the marker and tried to write. The feel of his skin, moist with sweat, made it almost impossible for me to remember my number. All I wanted was to press my face under his shirt. I managed to recall the necessary digits. My fingers brushed the edges of his nipple as I marked him. He trembled a little with each soft stroke. As I finished the last number, he leaned to lick the inside of my ear. "Go home and wait for my call." Then he buttoned up and left.

I sat there for a few minutes not moving. My cock was aching. And the wetness in my pants was becoming more visible. If I didn't leave soon, my juices would surely begin oozing straight through the fabric. I slowly stood up, not quite sure whether my legs would support me on my exit. As I passed through the door, I heard some commentary on my condition from the other customers. It didn't matter.

During the drive home I replayed our meeting and then started to worry. Would he call? Or would I be left alone again to take care of my own desires? Just as I got up to the front door, my telephone began to ring. I was trembling too much to work the key in the lock. When I finally banged the door open, I bolted for the phone. I reached it just in time to hear the receiver on the other end hang up. I slumped to the floor out of breath. I knew it was him and that he wouldn't call back. I leaned my head back against the couch.

Doug was by my side, looking at me with those brown eyes. He held up his drink. "A toast," he whispered, "to us and the incredible night we are about to experience." His tongue was deep inside my mouth once again. I hungered for it. I felt his breath against my neck as he caressed it with his lips. My balls pulled tight as he continued his way down my neck. His tongue circled my nipples before he bit them. The sensation was more than I had ever hoped to feel. My ears started to ring. The farther he went, the louder the ringing became. I knew I couldn't hold out much longer. My cock convulsed, ready to give in.

I awoke, startled. The ringing. I could still hear the ringing. It was the phone.

"Hello?"

"Kevin, it's Doug." The voice on the other end was music to my ears. "Listen, I'm ready and waiting for you. Just one thing before you come over. My dad's living with me for a while and he's downstairs watching television. When you come up to the front door, it'll be open. Come in and walk up the steps quietly. I'll be waiting in the third room on your right." I said nothing. I was still half in the dream. "Kevin, are you still there?"

"Sure, I'm here." I heard my voice cracking. I cleared it and tried again. "Won't you feel kind of awkward with your father there?"

"No, I've always wanted to have sex under my father's nose. You up for it or not?" I couldn't say no, not having gotten this close. I wanted to be near him. I needed to have him.

"Sure, I just need directions." The rest of our conversation was brief and to the point. I wrote down the directions and hung up the phone. I had told him I would be there within 30 minutes.

The drive was short as my mind played with the possibilities of the night. I looked at my watch as I pulled to a stop. Thirty-five minutes had passed since I spoke to Doug. I wondered what he was doing at that moment. And what would his father be doing? I began my approach to the opened door. As I got closer I could hear the television playing from somewhere in the house. I could only hope it was loud enough to cover up my intrusion. My heart hurt from the pounding. I opened the door carefully, expecting it to squeak. It was silent. I began inching toward the staircase, which was only a few feet in front of me. I felt like an actor in a horror movie where the exits keep getting farther and farther away. Just as I reached the stairs, the floor creaked from the next room. Then came the footsteps. I froze. I was in this strange house with no way out. The footsteps came closer; I was sure they were headed for me. I suddenly took the stairs two at a time. Once at the top I saw my door, my hideaway. I ran into the room and shut the door. Doug was lying there in his bed with only a small sheet to conceal his massive hard-on. "Your dad is coming up the stairs." I tried to catch my breath. Doug jumped out of bed, the look on his face pure excitement.

"Get in here," he said as he opened the closet door and pushed me in.

As I stood there in the dark trying to calm myself, I discovered that my cock was harder than it had ever been. Outside, I could hear Doug and his father chatting about going to bed. Inside, the smells of his closet were intense. I reached to my left and found his dress shirts. I imagined Doug as he removed them after a long day at work. I buried my face in them. My legs went weak. The conversation continued in his bedroom. I reached down and found his collection of shoes. I could smell the strong, wonderful smell inside them. Beside the shoes on the closet floor, there was one of his tank tops. I grabbed it with my free hand and rubbed it against the bulge in my pants. I forced myself to stop. I was ready to blow.

Suddenly the closet door opened. Doug found me with one of his shoes pressed up to my nose in one hand and holding on to his tank top with the other. A look of pleasure crossed his face as he showed every delicious inch of his body to me. He took the shoe from my hand and pushed his way into the closet with me. His mouth was immediately on me, biting my right nipple through the thin material of my shirt. I spread my legs apart so that his full body could rest against mine. My hand found its way to his enormous cock. He shivered at my touch. The air in the closet was now heavy, a mix of heat and sweat. His tongue probed my armpits as I continued my exploration of his damp crotch. His hairless balls hung low and pressed against my hand as my finger discovered his ass. He moaned with pleasure. We broke out of the closet.

We were all over each other, neither of us able to get enough of what we each wanted. I fell back against his bed, his hands tugging at my pants until they dropped on the floor. His body was on top of mine. Our cocks rubbed against each other, mixing their juices. He made his way down the entire length of my body until he found what he was searching for. My cock was immediately swallowed whole, and the warmth of his mouth made me gasp. I grabbed his hair. I began fucking his face, my cock going deeper inside his throat with each new thrust. I reached for his leg and pulled his body around. His ass was now within reach. He lowered himself as if begging me to enter him. My tongue sunk deep inside his tight hole. The taste was powerful. The aroma of his sweat and of soap surrounded me. Each time my tongue pierced the small pucker of his ass, the muscles would tighten, forcing me to withdraw. We played this little game for what seemed hours. By then the hair on his ass was soaked with my spit. He turned to face me. Tasting his own ass in my mouth, he began to suck the flavor off my tongue. His hair stuck to his face and neck with a mixture of sweat and the natural lube that was pouring out of my cock. I was crazed with desire. I had to have him in me.

Before I could speak, I heard footsteps in the hallway. Doug must have heard too because we both froze. The steps got louder. The door across the hall opened, then closed. We both lay there for a moment, making sure the old man was in for good. Then Doug lowered his head against my shoulder and whispered in my ear. "I want to make love to you now." He nibbled at my ear waiting for my reaction.

"I want to fuck you right here, right now, while my father is sleeping across the hall. I want to make you want to scream, when you know you can't for fear of waking him."

Within seconds he was above me, rubbing my ass with lube. Intense pain shot through me as his fingers found their way inside. I was terrified. If his fingers could cause that much pain, what in the hell would his enormous cock do? I tried to relax but couldn't. Doug saw the expression on my face, stopped with his fingers still inside me, and told me to relax. "Breathe deep. Don't fight it and just relax." He spoke softly to me. "That's better. Oh, yeah, I can feel your ass loosening." He slowly began moving his fingers inside of me. This time the pain was not as sharp. The feeling of his fingers leaving me made me cringe. My legs were now up over his shoulders. His cock glistened with his own sweet liquids. I could feel the large mushroom head pushing its way around the crack of my ass. It finally came to a stop, resting on the tight opening.

The pressure of having my ass invaded was heavy, but the head slid in with little pain. He slowly made another move, pushing even more of his cock into me. The pain shot again.

He bent over to kiss me, and my lips welcomed his. He pushed farther and then stopped, farther then stopped. I could feel his rod inside me, every inch of it moving deeper and deeper. At last he came to the base of his shaft. We lay there for a few moments. I have never forgotten that feeling of complete and total connection.

His hips began to move, backward and forward, as his cock slipped in and out of my burning ass. My hands groped for something to grip as the thrusts came more often, harder. I gripped the wooded rails of his headboard. I wanted to scream, but the thought of his father in the next room silenced me. Doug started to moan with pleasure, throwing his head back with each new push. I looked down and watched with amazement how easily his cock was moving in and out of me. He reached down between my legs, grabbed my cock, and began jerking me off. Either of the two acts was more than I had once wished for, but being fucked and jacked at the same time was maddening. I could feel my insides boiling, building up the pressure that was held in for so many years. My balls had tightened unbelievably. I reached down and grabbed them.

Doug released my dick, and I immediately took over. The feeling of my own hand was comforting. He spread my legs farther apart, his face strained with pressure. "Fuck, I'm going to shoot," he moaned.

"Yeah, give me your hot come! I want it all," I whispered hoarsely. Doug began to moan louder and louder. His thrusts were more violent. His chest glistened with sweat. His moans went higher pitched as he began to shoot. The warmth of his come rushed into me. Without realizing what was happening, I felt the warmth of my own come on my face. Doug kept pounding my ass, shooting more of his hot jizz into me. He finally collapsed on top of me. As we lay there, struggling for breath, he turned my head toward his and kissed me.

We must have fallen asleep in each other's arms. I woke up shortly before 4 in the morning. He held me tight, begged me not to go. But we knew all the same that I had to leave before his father woke up. We crept down the stairs, his hand entangled with mine. At the door, he promised me he would call.

"Thank you, Kevin, I can't tell you what last night meant to me," he whispered, softly laying another kiss on my lips. "I think I may have fallen in love with you. I have never felt like this before."

I looked at him and smiled. We kissed one last time. As I stepped out the door, I turned back. He was still standing there watching me with a smile and what I think was a tear on his cheek.

That was the last time I ever saw him. I don't know if his father found out. I don't know if he got scared because it was so strong. The only thing I'm sure of is that I was out of the closet for good. Oh, and I brought his tank top with me, stuffed in my back pocket. I'm not going to lose that.

Getting It Straight

Bob Condron

How many straight guys do you know who would ask you if they had a great ass? More than that, how many straight guys do you know who'd let you feel it in order to reach a decision? Well, Brian identifies himself as straight. And even as I'm holding and kneading his solid buttocks in my cupped palms he's telling me how his girlfriend tells him that he has a cute behind, but he would like some confirmation.

And all this in public. We're at a party, standing in the hallway. Mutual friends and acquaintances pass by and look on in shock and amusement, but he is somehow oblivious.

"Brian, that is one great ass," I tell him.

"Really? Are you sure?" he asks.

"Believe me. I am something of a butt connoisseur. And I can tell you in all sincerity that you have one fabulous ass!"

Somehow he fails to see the humor in the situation and keeps a straight face. Deadly serious. "Honestly? That's good to know. 'Cause, I mean, I don't know." Then he volunteers the information, almost apologetically, "But it's really hairy."

"That is nothing to be ashamed of," I assure him. "A big solid hairy butt looks good on a man. Especially one as cute and chunky as you. Want to show it to me? I'd be happy to reassure you some more."

There's a brief moment while I watch the cogs turn and his mind click into gear and then, "Nice try!" he says with a sardonic grin. "Maybe next time."

"Whenever you're ready," I add as I stroll toward the bar in the kitchen for another margarita.

Fifteen minutes later I am surrounded by a group of friends. They are laughing and joking. Me? I'm kind of camouflaged. Watching Brian at the other end of the spacious kitchen. He's too melancholy and introspective to notice my gaze. Kristina appears to be doing her damnedest to cheer him up.

He doesn't notice my taking him in. All of him. Three quarters Sicilian, one quarter Irish. The best of both worlds. Short, muscular, and stocky. Big doe eyes and long lashes. Close-cropped black hair and a goatee. A forest of chest hair tufting out of the V neck of his T-shirt.

Finally, she calls it quits and walks over toward our little clique as he disappears into his daiquiri.

"What's his problem?" I ask.

"Can't you guess?" she replies, rolling her eyes heavenward. "Louise," she says matter-of-factly, "always Louise. The little princess."

"Where is she tonight?"

"Out with the girls." She purses her lips tightly. "He's totally jealous, and she doesn't help matters. It's like, last week we were at a party and she suddenly announces to the room that she met a guy in a club who—" and here Kristina does her hilarious impression of Louise's cut-glass accent, "—'asked me to take my knickers down and give them to him. So…I did!' You should have seen his face. He had steam coming out of his ears! He went ballistic. I don't know who is worse. Him or her."

"Definitely her," I reply. "At least he's cute!" And with this, I toast her with my glass and cross the crowded room to Brian's side.

"So, Brian, how goes it?"

"Not so good. Not so bad."

"And Louise?"

"Who?" he grimaces, then shrugs it off, changing the subject. "You mind if I ask you a personal question?"

"Ask away."

"How long have you known you were gay?"

"Can't think of a time when I didn't know."

"And you're happy?"

"Remarkably. And you?"

"And me what?"

"When did you realize you were gay?"

"Me?" He lets out a nervous snort. "I'm not gay. I'm as straight as they come!"

"Really?"

"Yeah, really. But don't get me wrong, I don't have a problem with it. My brother's gay."

I place my tongue firmly in my cheek. "So is he as handsome as you?"

Once again he fails to see the joke and answers me in all seriousness. "Some people say the resemblance is amazing, but others don't see it at all."

"You don't get it, do you, Brian?"

"Eh?"

I pry the empty glass from his grip and hold it up at eye level. "Time for a refill?"

By the time I return he's nowhere to be seen. I check my watch. It's almost 3 in the morning.

"Great party, Kristina," I tell her as I hand her the drinks and kiss her good night on both cheeks in the continental fashion. "Had a great time."

She sees me to the door and waves me good-bye as I stumble down the stairwell.

Outside, the night air is unusually mild. I skip down the front steps to find Brian sitting at the bottom, head in hands. Lost in thought.

"Going some place or just taking in the night air?" I ask.

"Steeling myself to head home," he replies.

"Don't like the idea?"

"No enthusiasm. And no cab in sight." He glances up and down the deserted street.

"I live just around the corner, Brian. You can crash at my place if you like?"

"OK," he says, standing.

No resistance; his complicity takes me by surprise. Nothing more to be said, we set off in the direction of home.

I close the front door behind us and throw the bolt.

"Coffee?"

"Bed," he replies, matter-of-factly.

I lead him through to the spare room and switch on the bed-side lamp as he peels the T-shirt over his head.

Pointing to the bed, I tell him, "You sleep here. You need anything, I'm just next door."

"Don't leave me!" he whines, yanking off one boot. "Stay and talk awhile."

"Want a bedtime story?"

He pouts in response.

"OK, OK! I'll get a coffee and be back," I promise him.

When I return he's already in bed. I sit on the floor alongside the bed, my back pressed up against the wall, coffee at my side.

"This bed is so comfortable," he declares, stretching out like a cat. "*So* comfortable."

I can't help but chuckle. He sounds just like a kid.

"I used to cuddle up to my big brother in bed when I was little and upset."

Why is he telling me this? "You upset now?"

"Some." He throws back the duvet and rolls around. And he's stark naked. His thick, tubular cock and heavy balls slap his hairy thighs as he contorts his sturdy physique first this way, then that. "This bed is *so* fucking comfortable. So comfortable."

I'm laughing again. He covers himself once more.

"I don't like to see you down there," he says, almost as an aside. "Take your clothes off and get in with me."

He doesn't need to ask me twice. Within moments I've stripped naked and stand over him, my cock semierect. My fists clench and release. Resting on one elbow, he looks up into my face and turns back the corner of the duvet. I slide in beside him, the bedsheet feeling cool against my skin, and, all at once, he launches himself at me. His strong arms coil around me, his beefy legs clasp me in a vicelike grip. He snuggles into the nape of my neck.

"This is so lovely," he coos. "So lovely."

Holding him tightly in my arms, I'm wondering about this seemingly effortless shift from straight to gay. It feels mildly ridiculous. No more than a couple of hours ago he was adamant. Now he's behaving like it's all second nature. But I'm not so dumb as to challenge him. At least, not at this moment. I take his chin in my hand, turn his mouth upward, and smother his moist, open mouth with my own.

His tongue hesitates, then probes into the depths between my yawning lips. His body writhes against mine. I hold him tight, clutching at his hairy buttocks, feeling his cock unfurl and grow hard as granite, pressing against my belly now. The sodden tip leaves a silver snail's trail over my skin as he wriggles against the flat of my stomach. My dick is just as rigid as his.

"This feels good," he mumbles.

"Uh-huh."

"I said, 'This feels good.'" His voice sounds suddenly bolder.

"Yeah. Feels real good. And your ass, Brian—" I punctuate the sentence with a little squeeze, "could win prizes!"

He finally recognizes a joke and giggles. His laughter is charming. Charming and somehow full of innocence.

"Feels good to have your hands on me. Skin against skin. Feels so good."

"Let me look at you," I say, throwing back the duvet.

He rolls over onto his belly as I spring to my knees. Looking down at him now from this vantage point I can see all, like an eagle readying itself to swoop: head resting on arms folded across the feather pillow, the breadth of his back splayed against cream sheets, exquisite lines leading down to a narrow waist, and then the deep tan line framing his pale, hairy butt. A sumptuous butt. Good enough to eat. The cleft deep and dark. Full of mystery. Begging to be explored.

I place my hands on his waist and flip him over. He relaxes back, grinning, enjoying my enjoying him. Breathing deep. The expanse of his hairy chest swelling as he inhales, his cock twitching, straining up toward his navel. Legs crossed at the ankles.

"You just going to look?" he finally asks.

I clasp my fist around his cock and squeeze, watching precome seep from the deep slit in the rose-pink tip. I stretch out my thumb and spread the translucent goo over the smooth, tender surface. He shudders and moans, grinding his hips up toward me.

"Please," he growls, his throat thick with desire. Just that, "Please—"

Tongue replaces thumb, lapping at the swollen helmet, tracing its velvety contours, running around the rim, the bulbous head bordering on the succulent shaft. And then I consume him in a single gulp, my nose pressing against his fertile balls, pubic hair tickling my nostrils.

His response is immediate. Pulling me down toward him, he raises himself up to swallow my sword. Next thing you know we're burning the candle at both ends. What he lacks in experience he more than makes up for with enthusiasm.

Five? Ten? Fifteen minutes? I could taste his dick for hours. It fills my mouth, my throat, feeds my appetite. Yet I hunger always for more. Chewing and suckling on the supple flesh. Gagging on the solid core. My fingers cut a swath through his forested crack and meet their objective, teasing his ring as I continue to feast.

"Come," he's begging me. "Please!"

"What's your hurry?" I gasp, and then it becomes clear.

"Can't hold off any longer. It's going to blow. Any second now, it's going to blow. Has to. Here it comes, brother. Here it comes. Coming now. Coming—"

With a whimper, the first spasm produces just a tremor. The second, a low moan and a glob that oozes from the slit and over the tip. But with the third comes a toe-curling whoop, and his solid manhood spurts like a fountain. A thick rope of come flies high in the air and splatters on his quivering belly. Then, again and again. Three powerful spurts collectively forming a thick, creamy pool. He shoots a couple more times but less intensely. Rivulets of sperm dribble over my fingers, ebbing away, draining the tension away.

But not for me. No. Fuck no. Now it's my turn. I'm wound up like a top and ready to let fly. My nuts hunker up high, and with a whoosh the deluge of molten sperm begins to erupt. Cascading over his tits and belly. Spraying onto his neck. Each squirt intensely felt as come rises from my sac and surges through my aching tubes. He reaches up a hand to cup my balls tenderly and shakes the last few drops free from the tip. The final drop splashes onto his chin. I wipe it away with my finger, wipe my finger on the sheet.

We crumple up into a single heap. He sighs, and in so doing, his body seems to melt against me. I kiss his slack, salty ball sac.

"Sleep?"

"I can come three times," he tells me.

I pause. "Are you bragging or complaining?"

He laughs once more, delighted. "That's for you to decide."

"OK—" I chuckle drowsily. "Just give me five minutes."

Paradise Falls

B.B. Wills

*A*ustralia is wonderful, from Sydney's white arched opera house to the coral caves of the Great Barrier Reef to the white sand of the beaches. And along with the natural beauty of those beaches are the Aussie lifeguards that we've all seen on calendars and postcards.

Cody guarded the beachfront that I enjoyed most. I'm not sure if I enjoyed it more for the beach itself or for Cody. He was a spectacular specimen of a man, especially in his tiny Speedo. Standing 6 foot 3 with a lean and thickly muscled body from his calves to his 17-inch neck, topped off with a head full of wind-tossed hair bleached by sun and salt water, he could inspire lesser men (like me) to consider faking drowning in the hope that he would deliver mouth-to-mouth resuscitation.

As it happened, we met on the first day of my vacation when the undertow was stronger than I expected and I had to be rescued. By Cody. He swam out to me without any hesitation or fear and instructed me to wrap my arms around his neck and ride in on his back as he headed for the shore. Mouth-to-mouth wasn't necessary—unfortunately—but he did pull my left arm across his shoulders and wrap his strong hand completely around my wrist. Gripping my waist with his right arm, he carried me without effort to the warm, soft sand and gently put me down. As he was crouching down on one knee next to me, I had an unobstructed view of his substantial cock and balls, which created a colorful bulge between his thighs. I slowly scanned up a broad, hairless, ribbed abdomen, complete with an innie belly button above the top of his Speedo that anchored the perfect center line of his evenly muscled chest. Beautifully defined pecs, which would easily cast a shadow over his stomach on the cloudiest day, were capped by large brown nipples. His hands were large and had bulging blue veins that ran up his thick and muscled forearms. Biceps about 14 inches around were capped by broad, hard, muscled shoulders and a thick neck. His face was clean-shaven, and his thin, sensuous lips revealed perfect white-as-snow teeth. His hazel eyes reflected the blues and greens of the ocean water, and his short spiked hair was shaved close on the sides. A single gold hoop earring glistened in the sun. My mind flashing in and out of various fantasies, I didn't hear him ask if I was all right until he grasped my shoulders and leaned in closer to ask again. Snapping back to reality, I assured him that I was OK, and he helped me to my feet. With a warm smile, he went back to his lifeguard station and I to my blanket.

Each day I made my way back to the beach and set up camp closer and closer to Cody's station. Although his greetings got friendlier and our conversations longer as the many days went by, he didn't send off any vibes that set off my gaydar.

With just one day left before my departure to New Zealand, Cody accepted my invitation to have dinner. We met at a small intimate neighborhood restaurant that was a favorite of the locals and not at all known by the tourists. The fresh seafood, prepared in an unpretentious way, relied upon its own delicious flavor instead of overpowering sauces and spices. We languished over our wine and talked as if we were lifelong friends. Without any hesitation, I accepted his invitation to his place for a night-cap. His apartment was compact and neat, with an alcove just large enough to fit his king-size bed. Cody disappeared into the bathroom and reappeared in a tank top and cutoff sweatpants that seemed just long enough in the leg to cover his penis. We sat on the sofa, which was barely large enough for two full-size men. As the wine continued to relax us, our knees slowly came together, followed by more and more of our thighs. As he shift-ed, the sweatpants finally revealed a large mushroom-capped cock head. Whether it was the wine or the fact that I was leav-ing the next morning, I got brave and decided to take matters into my own hands, so to speak. I slid my hand onto his smooth-ly muscled thigh. There was no reaction from him except for a definite jump of the bulge between his legs. I ran my hand up the inside of his thigh, touching his skin lightly enough to cause goose bumps across his body. I pushed the fabric aside and allowed his flaccid prick and soft ball sac to roll out and rest on the seat cushion.

As I lowered myself onto my knees between his massive thighs, he slouched down on the couch so that his thickening cock hung down toward the floor, just off the edge of the couch. The only hair on his body was the lush bush above the base of his penis. His cock was nestled against an ample sac that held two walnut-size testicles hanging about two inches below the head of his cock. As I sucked him deep into the back of my mouth, he removed his shirt and began working his big brown nipples with both his hands. My oxygen supply was soon cut off as I played one of my greatest symphonies on his skin flute with my tongue. Pulling back, I wrapped my hand around the base of his tool and worked the engorged head with my mouth. I went down on his balls and sucked one and then the other into my mouth, moving back and forth from one to the other as he moaned softly. I focused my hungry mouth on that tender spot of skin, behind his ball sac, that thinly covers the root of the penis and makes a bridge between the ball sac and the hole that provides so much pleasure. As I nibbled and sucked it, Cody moaned louder and began gyrating his hips slowly.

I went back up to his plum-colored cock head that proudly stood atop eight inches of throbbing flesh. I licked up the sides to the piss slit, which now oozed precome. His nipples stood out about two inches from his chest and were supersensitized as he continued to work them between his forefingers and thumbs. I eased his full eight inches into my mouth and went back to sucking him with all I had. His breathing became shallow and his moaning became louder as his hips began thrusting upward to meet my downward motion. His cock got as rigid as a tall oak and the flared edges of the engorged head sent electric charges through my body. His first shot of hot, salty come hit the back of my throat. I continued swallowing, gulping to keep up with wave after wave of the hot liquid. When his body tremors stopped I sucked the last drop out of him, savoring this once-in-a-lifetime pleasure, as I feverishly stroked my own cock until I shot my load up onto his thighs.

Landing in New Zealand early the next day, I followed Cody's directions to one of the most beautiful forest spots in the world.

Lush tropical greenery surrounded pools of crystal-clear blue water, which sat below cascading waterfalls. With gently falling waters, walking across the rocks allowed visitors to move in and out of the waterfall, actually standing behind the sheet of water, invisible from the outside world. I spread out on a large rock to enjoy the sun and awoke sometime later. Heading into the pool of cool refreshing water, I caught a glimpse of someone venturing behind the waterfall. Always curious, I followed along. As I perched on a rock, deafened by the roar of the falling water, I glimpsed him from behind, carefully placing his clothes on a rock to keep dry. When he stood, my eyes feasted on 6 feet 4 inches of living, breathing god. Long dark brown hair rested on his shoulders. A broad back tapered to a tight V around his waist. His ass cheeks, covered in a soft blanket of dark hair, were firm and round like two halves of a volleyball. They led down to thick thighs and muscled calves that continued the dark blanket of fur down to his feet. He turned to face my way, still unaware of my presence, and raised his arms straight up above his head, to stretch his massive body. With his arms outstretched, his pits had thick bushes of dark hair.

His shoulders were wide and ended in well-rounded muscle caps. At 18 inches, his unflexed biceps made Cody's look small. His thick forearms and wrists supported two massive hands with each finger large enough to fuck me into ecstasy. His chest rhythmically rose and fell as his lungs filled with air, expanding his large pecs. His chest was covered in a lush blanket of dark hair from his Adam's apple to the bush above his cock. His abs were so rippled that even the mat of hair didn't hide them from view. The uncut prize package hanging between his legs made me gasp. Thickly hanging toward his feet about five inches in length, it rested against a hairy sac holding two plum-size nuts. He slowly ran his hands down his chest, crisscrossing them to run his strong fingers over every inch of his chest. He lingered at his nipples as he grasped them between forefinger and thumb and squeezed them tightly. He continued downward with his right hand until he slide his fingers through his crouch and under his ball sac. He wrapped his hand around the slowly thickening shaft and began stroking himself. As his cock filled with blood, it got thicker and longer. He worked the skin hood up and down the entire length of the shaft, allowing a bell-shaped hood to peek in and out. As he stroked himself his balls swung back and forth freely between his legs.

I removed my shorts and took hold of my own hardening prick to match the speed of his strokes. Soon he threw his head all the way back and closed his eyes. He growled a deep, low, animalistic sound and shot a stream of come straight out into the wall of water just ahead of him. Two, then three shots of hot liquid, then a few more strokes of his huge hand, ensured that his balls were empty. I continued to pump my tool as he stepped forward into the spray of the waterfall. He turned to back into the waterfall, and as it hit his uplifted face, it slowly cascaded over his heaving chest, matting down his lush blanket of hair. He rubbed his body with his hands, ensuring that his cock head was rinsed clean. As he stepped forward, the water dripped slowly off his long hair and trickled down his chest, drops lingering on his nipples. As he ran his hands up his body, brushing the water off his hair, it once again stood out like a soft, fluffy rug.

As I was about to come, the chimes rang out, signaling to the stewardess it was time to instruct us to raise our seats and tray tables for landing in New Zealand. Snapping out of my daydream, I realized that the first thing I needed to do after landing was head to Paradise Falls.

Love in the Midnight Sun

Kevin J. Olomon

September can bring a slight chill in the air as the sun finally begins to set, bringing darkness to the Alaskan sky after a summer of midnight sun. Still, the air in the cabin seems far too cold to be warmed by a mere fire as I poke at the logs hiding the smoking, crackling red embers. This lofty log room, smelling of matches and smoke, hasn't felt this lonely all summer, and now even the shadows in the corners seem darker than they were only yesterday. Kindling this fire, I try to bring back some of the warmth that left my cabin when I took Matthew to the airport in town. This send-off was sorrowful, though I tried not to show how his leaving was emptying me of my spirit and diminishing my hope of ever finding love in the frozen north.

Matthew and I met early that summer as the busy tourist season at the wilderness lodge down the mountain from my home started up. He had traveled north for adventure, from Portland, on his summer break from school. I was on summer vacation as well from my teaching position up in Anchorage, supplementing my income by filling in as a lecturing naturalist and guide at the lodge. I spent my days answering the questions of elderly cruise ship passengers awaiting their flights back to the Lower 48 after a glamorous, buffet-filled sail up the Last Frontier State's Inside Passage. Matthew passed his days as a bartender, charming big tips out of the lodge guests as they lounged riverside, admiring the catches of the salmon fishermen.

Matthew is a nice-looking college boy, slight of build, probably not 130 pounds, with strawberry-blond hair and always sporting a half smile. He was a charmer, and many times I found him carrying up the rear of the groups I led down the nature trails, pointing out the purple lupine and pink fireweed in full bloom, along with the brambles of blueberries, low-bush cranberries, and tracks belonging to moose and brown bear.

We were on the bluff overlooking the rolling rapids, emerald-green from thousands of years of glacial silt deposited on the river bottom. Silently, I wondered why this handsome young man might be tagging along so often on these tours with these slower older folks whose endless questions even I grew tired of hearing over and over again. Lately, I had begun to notice that he was carefully attentive to the pearl-haired ladies toward the rear of the group as they strained to hear my sometimes too soft answers to questions they had also wanted to ask. I realized that he was assisting in making sure they heard and understood my explanations and soon, they were turning to him instead of me for answers to their queries on the trail. He'd heard my standard answers so many times he could easily recite them. His patience with the ladies was rewarded with ruby-lipped pecks on the cheek as he led them arm in arm down the stony path.

At the crest of the bluff in a stand of birch trees, he looked up at me as I was explaining the mating ritual of the bald eagle to some of the husbands up front. The regal birds, in courtship, flew together up in the sky as high as they could before locking talons and free-falling, joining bodies and completing the act of intimacy, then separating just in time, as their fall brought them dangerously close to the rocky cliffs. He smiled at the gasps from the group. Our eyes met, and he tilted his head, seeming to marvel at my storytelling and my enthusiasm with these old folks' interest.

Back at the lodge, I escorted the last gray-haired couple into the gift shop so that the staff there could talk them into making a purchase. I leaned against an umbrella table on the deck, searching for my handkerchief to wipe a bead of sweat from my tan brow in the hot midday sun. Dressed in an olive polo shirt and khaki shorts, my broad-built 6-foot 210-pound frame was warming even more as I was joined by a silent, smiling Matthew. His fingers beat my handkerchief to my forehead, catching in their swipe the beads of sweat I'd wanted to wipe. He handed me his frosty soda can, and I took a swig. "They're nuts about you, y'know," he said, his hair shining scarlet in the June sun.

As I tried not to melt in his gaze, I asked, "Just like you, huh?" He broke his stare with me and looked to the deck, mumbling something that he wasn't ready for me to hear. I felt a flutter of bravery from somewhere inside my chest and, not caring who might see, I placed a firm grasp around his wrist and softly said, "At least I'm hoping you've got a thing for me, handsome man."

That night we met at the summer solstice party of off-duty lodge staff at a sandy stretch of shoreline down along the river.

After enjoying some light guitar strumming before the bonfire, and a supper of fresh-caught king salmon and icy brew, I made my way through some brush down to the floating dock, hoping Matthew would follow. Unable to hear his approach as the rapids crashed by, I felt his warm breath on the center of my back, through the thin shirt I was wearing. Turning to him and seeing his lips move but still unable to hear for the water, I bent into his neck, placing my ear at his mouth's level, and he nuzzled his stubbly chin into the hollow of my throat. He cooed like a dove and wriggled in my firm grasp as I licked the vein trailing from his ear down along his jawline. Then I softly blew my breath onto his moist skin, sending through him a chill, then a shiver, from which I would rescue him with a tight embrace. As we coupled, a coworker who'd sneaked onto the dock, sensing the readiness of our moment, slid his Jeep keys into my pocket and patted my rump, giving me the go-ahead to use his rig to transport this young man away.

Once home, on the stairs leading up to the loft, I led the way clad only in flannel boxers. Matthew was at my heels with his hand tucked into the back of my waistband. He seemed groggy and tired yet excited and full of anticipation of the lovemaking we both had planned. Backing him into the raised footboard of my timber-frame bed, I placed my hands in his warm under-arms to lift his small body into my much larger mass. My head instinctively rolled into my shoulder, and Matthew took the cue and attacked my neck with his warm, wet mouth. I couldn't tell which of us was the one breathing heavily as I mumbled to him that I hadn't made love in nearly a full year, so that he might know that it was not part of my character to do this with just anyone. He gasped between assaults with his powerful mouth, then curled into my chest as I thought I heard him say, "I've never done this before." He stood up straight, looked into my face, and reached with his pink fingertips to brush a tear from my cheek that I hadn't known was there.

Forcing him onto his back against the white down duvet on the mattress, my hands held his wrists pinned at the headboard. My tongue danced wildly, dipping in and out of his mouth, twirling with his own tongue and sucking his lips. We kissed for what seemed like half the night, writhing, our skin warm against the cool of the sheets. We never grew tired but only advanced, looking forward to further lovemaking but never hurrying to it. I felt my expanding hardness pressing against the wet, soggy cotton of my boxers and also felt Matthew's hard fullness straining under me. My mouth left his, my breath meandering down the cleft in his chin, past the mole on his neck, across his shapely smooth chest, to sink in the silky soft hair of his armpit. As he gasped quietly, I breathed in his light young scent, licking, starving for more of his taste. I crossed to his hard nipple. He attempted to pull his wrists from my hold as my teeth sank into his skin, my chin quivering as I bit into his flesh. Matthew cried out as I continued biting down, forcing his nipple to realize that it had never before been bitten. Then, this small man did something that totally shocked me. With one swift, fluid move, his tiny frame broke from my grip and reversed our positions so that he now straddled atop my body, which was twice his in both weight and mass. He sat on the tight skin of my hairy belly as he held my forearms down by my navel, close to his ass. Taking a moment to catch his breath after that last amazing move, he smiled slyly, staring deep into my eyes.

"So now what, little man?" I demanded, returning his stare and his sneer.

He leaned forward, gently caressing the dark fur on my chest and belly and spread airy kisses all across my face as he said, "I have neither a plan nor a desire for what we are up to, to be over quickly." Pulling forward, as he had, to make up for our differences in height, reaching my face with his, his rump raised off my stomach somewhat. My hungry fingers took advantage of the space they'd been awarded and sneaked into his private areas up through the legs of his briefs, and in one tug they were yanked down across his plump ass, then down his legs and inside out as they were flung across the loft. My exploring fingers went first to my wet mouth, then retraced the trail down to this dear man's lower regions and probed their way past his dangling ball sac to home in on the moist, soft skin of his spread ass. My fingers gently, delicately teased the hairs around his hole as my thumb zeroed in on the weakness of the warm, wet center. Matthew's sucking, nibbling mouth left my neck as his back violently arched, not in pain but in serious pleasure, as my thumb let itself into the silky, wet confines of the muscle ring just inside his warmth. He moaned uncontrollably, flexing his torso as my thumb twisted deeper into him, entering that space of roominess just past his sphincter, seeking out his spongy knob of soft flesh that would shoot bolts of energy through his body, once pressed upon. All the while his slightly curved hefty cock leaked precome onto my belly. My left hand smeared in the liquid and lifted to Matthew's mouth, and he sucked the salty syrup from my fingers.

By this time my own cock was wet and aching to be in Matthew's mouth. I removed my thumb from his butt with a soft, wet sound and slid his hot body down mine until his lips were working my cock head furiously. Before I realized what was happening, my entire cock, modest in length, but impressive in girth, was swallowed entirely by this beauty. His slippery tongue slithered from side to side a hundred miles an hour, bathing the underside of my meat in a foam of slobber as his lips slowly slid back up to the bulging head and slowly back down again. His technique of combining hard, speedy tongue movements with deliberately slow up-and-down motions made my back arch and my head spin. His throat was warm and velvety as his teeth gently grazed the crown of my cock head. My fingers tangled into his red hair and gently tugged at its softness. His sloppy mouth sounds added to the sudden realization that not only was I in the mouth of the most beautiful man I had ever made love to, but I was also sharing my body with a man whom I wanted to never stop being with. His lovemaking was so intense as he went down on me that I felt like he was swallowing, in fact consuming, my entire body from head to toe. Every part of my body that could grow hard with energy and stimulation was throbbing at this point. Even my insides seemed to participate in the joy and sensation that Matthew was treating my skin to.

In the dimming dusklike light of the North Country midnight hour, unable to wait any longer, I cupped his beautiful face in my huge hands and pulled him back up my torso to my own face. After a deep kiss, tasting myself back in the far reaches of his mouth, I asked if I could fuck him. He climbed off me and crawled toward the edge of the bed on all fours. The he reached up with both hands and hugged the vertical pine post of the timber frame, flexing his well-defined back muscles and poking his pale butt as far into the air as it would go. Never had anything looked so desperate for love and attention to me. I crawled to him on my knees and took a handful of his ass in each palm, spreading him wide open. His pink hole glistened, moist and clean. I lowered my face to his skin, breathing him in and smelling his body, rubbing my nose and chin into his crease. He moaned aggressively, shoving his bucking butt onto me. My tongue broke into his entry, feeling his softness and tasting his musk. Bathing his hole in spit, my tongue slid in and out, brushing the walls of his ass with the juice of my mouth. He reached back with his left hand, pushing his long middle finger into himself as my tongue competed for space.

Losing my tamed patience, I removed my face from Matthew's sweet ass and prepared my body for entry into his. I pushed the head of my drooling cock at the door of his spongy ass and leaned forward, being led through its suppleness by the squeezing, milking movements of his hungry butt. All the way in, unbelievable was his warmth and the silkiness of his insides. As he gripped the bedpost and I held onto him in a similar fashion, I plunged roughly and deeply into him and back out again as his moans and my growls sang in unison. The hot, wet intensity of our bodies worked together to achieve a heightened state of ecstasy that kept my mind in a swirling frenzy of heat and movement. Finally, unable to endure the pleasure-pain of friction any longer, I withdrew from him, and he quickly flipped onto his back, lifting his heels to my shoulders. Tugging on his own penis as he exploded gobs of gooey semen onto his own belly and chest, his tits heaving with every breath he took, he closed his eyes, and his face contorted into a look of exasperated release. Smelling the saltiness of his fluid took me over the edge, pumping my own dick with my tight fist. My first shot leaped from me and slammed across his face as I aimed lower so that my next shots sputtered out, mingling my come with Matthew's on his skin. With heaving breaths, I shook the come from my cock and placed my soaked palm flat on his stomach, rubbing his abs in a circular motion, collecting our semen on my hands and fingers. I raised my hand to my mouth, smelling the sweetness of our combined love as Matthew sighed at the sight of me licking our seed from my skin. The taste on my tongue was pungent and creamy as it dissolved on my palate. Smiling, he tugged at my wrist, lowering my palm to his own lips as he shared in the sampling of our taste.

I collapsed onto Matthew and ground my body into his, mixing our sperm, sweat, and saliva. I stretched my arms around the broadest section of his heaving chest so that my still touch would affect as much of his body as possible as we slept. I held Matthew in that man-to-man embrace through the remainder of our first night together that solstice evening.

Kneeling before the hearth now, the fire flaming and crackling, the smoke tickling my nostrils as my teary eyes distort the orangeness of the up-reaching flames, my arms long for the warm flesh they had grown used to encircling this summer. Never had time passed so quickly and never has this cabin felt so empty. My bare feet pad across the plank floor where I plant myself on the sofa. I wipe my eyes with a corner of the down comforter—the one that still holds the memorable musky scent of our last nights together.

Cool Shirt

A.J. Arweson

I was hanging out at Lucy's Let's Drop Inn, just checking out the scene. Lucy's is out in the hills beyond the edge of town, just up the road from St. Andrew's College and a couple of miles from El Toro, the big Marine air base. Lucy's used to be a big Marine hangout, back before they started shutting El Toro down. Usually there are a few kids from St. Andrew's, not the party crowd, just the types who like to have a beer with the townies. Some nights, a couple of El Toro jarheads end up at Lucy's, the ones who just want to get drunk by themselves or hope they'll get lucky with a coed from St. Andrews or just aren't up to the drive into town.

The Marines and the college kids mix in just fine with the neighborhood regulars, the low-grade alcoholics who always seem to have a drink in one hand and a cigarette in the other. A Seberg 400 jukebox loaded with 45s that haven't been changed in 30 years sits in the corner. The Marines and the college kids can be counted on to part with a few quarters, providing about all the sorry energy that Lucy's can muster. The energy sure doesn't come from Sam, the fat bartender. Sam just stands behind his shiny mahogany bar looking glum. For Sam, a surly "What'll you have?" is a long conversation.

Sam's attitude doesn't seem to hurt business much. And Lucy's Let's Drop Inn doesn't have a high-tipping crowd, so it doesn't hurt his income either. The $5 or so I slip him every now and then buys an extra measure of tolerance, just in case I want some privacy with a prospect or feel like getting into something maybe a little out of the ordinary. It's not a real promising scene, but you never know. Sometimes I get lucky and work up a little action. I ordered a Rolling Rock. Sam grumbled as he rummaged in the cooler. It was easier to serve a Bud.

Anyway, it was a slow Tuesday night. Sad country-western ballads on the jukebox were about the best thing going, so you can see how slow it was.

Except for this one thing. A blond kid over in the corner was trying to flirt with three uninterested St. Andrew's girls, real cool-like. But he was just a redneck Okie with a Marine buzzcut on his knobby head and attitude picked up from being 90 days out of boot camp. Still, it was fun watching him practicing his newfound military manhood. He was the only guy in the place worth looking at. It sure wasn't Sam in his yellow-stained T-shirt, and it sure wasn't the lonely alcoholic sitting on the corner barstool knocking down boilermakers.

I sat there, nursing my beer, watching the kid trying to make time with the three bored girls. The kid got up to get a beer. I didn't know it, but I was about to get lucky. I still wasn't all that interested.

The kid's body was nice enough, lean with just enough padding of new muscles over his bones, courtesy of hormones and the drill sergeant. He had good arms, not quite big enough to stretch out the sleeves on his T, but they had potential. He had full lips, kind of tender and vulnerable looking. But when you came down to it, he was just another inexperienced kid. He had this weird lanky loping walk. He swung his long skinny arms back and forth like he was on a 20-mile hike, like it wasn't only six or seven steps to the bar.

I was over dealing with kids. And since this kid was the only guy worth looking at that night, it looked like I was going to leave Lucy's and drive alone back up to my place in the Santa Ana foothills. Trooper and Sarge, my golden labs, would be glad to have me home early.

I said I didn't have much interest in the kid, but he had this cool olive-brown T-shirt, a redneck sort of shirt. The cheap washed-out cotton draped over his bony shoulders and showed off the budding muscles on his flat chest. No-show nipples. At least for now.

The T-shirt looked good, but the best thing about the shirt was the logo. The words *power back* were strung out in block letters above a heavy black rectangle resting on two short squares. Kind of like a bench you might want to do some serious industrial work on. The shirt hung loose on the kid but looked just right for me. Probably snug enough to do a good job of showing off my chest next time I showed up at the Anvil.

I wanted that shirt.

The kid walked up to the bar with his odd lanky stride and came to a halt next to me at the bar.

Sam managed to separate himself from the far end of the bar and asked, "What'll you have?"

"A Bud," the kid answered. A good choice. Buds were easy to find. The kid pulled a crumpled single and three quarters out of his pocket and laid them carefully on the bar. The hair on his forearms was bleached gold against his reddish tanned skin.

Nice forearms. Nice skin. I looked over his way while Sam ambled over to the cooler.

"Cool shirt," I said, looking first at the kid's chest, then down at my beer.

"Beg pardon, sir?" he answered, looking over at me. Nice touch, the sir. Promising.

"I said, 'Nice shirt.'" I turned my head his way and looked him square in the face. My green eyes into his pale blues. "Twenty bucks for the shirt."

The kid's eyes widened into a deer-in-the-headlight gaze, then dropped to the floor. His ruddy cheeks got ruddier, right down his neck and under the cool shirt. His short, narrow life hadn't prepared the kid for a proposition so off-the-wall. Sam came over with the Bud and took the buck seventy-five. When it looked like Sam wasn't going anywhere, I laid a ten spot on the counter and suggested that the guy at the other end of the bar was looking kind of thirsty. Sam grunted, took the money, and took himself off.

The kid stood there hanging onto the bottle of Bud like it was a life preserver. He shifted back and forth on his big feet, revving up to bolt back to the safety of the trio of coeds. The coeds stood in their little pack, silent as lambs, watching us.

The kid turned to go. But I wasn't ready to give up. I grabbed him by the arm and pulled his arm up against my chest. "Hell, it's a real cool shirt. Make it 40," I said. I was so close he could feel the heat of my breath against his neck.

The kid gulped down a swig of beer. He was having a tough time keeping his boot-camp cool. I pulled two crisp 20s out of my pocket and laid them on the bar.

The kid looked across the bar and checked himself out in the mirror. He shrugged and somehow managed to find his way back to his cool military dude with a Bud attitude. He looked over at me and laughed.

"Shit," he said, "the fucking T is yours man. Let's go outside. We can trade shirts there." The Marine Corps isn't a high-paying operation. He could use the money.

He must have decided I was harmless.

Wrong.

Now the kid was acting a little too cool. I liked him better when he was nervous. I generally like my men nervous. If I was going to part with 40 bucks, I might as well have a little fun. So I stared him down just the way I had every other punk I'd met since I was a punk myself.

"That's OK," I said. "No need to step outside. And no trade. My 40 bucks for your shirt. We can close the deal right here. Take off your shirt and hand it over. There's the money, right there on the bar."

Lucky for me none of his buddies were there. I wouldn't have had a chance. The strategic advantage was definitely on my side. I was older, bigger, half a head taller, and I had the 40 bucks. Now the kid was nice and nervous. There were as many beads of sweat forming on his forehead as there were on the bottle of Bud clenched in his fist.

Lucy's isn't the kind of place that has dim atmospheric lighting. He'd be standing in the bar bare-chested in front of Sam and the coeds and the alcoholics. I wanted to laugh watching him try to think it over. It was a pretty clear situation; analysis wasn't this particular Marine's strong point.

But he'd have the 40 bucks.

Things were definitely getting better. I could smell the fear radiating from the kid's armpits. Delicious, the smell of fear. Almost as good as the smell of lust. The kid hesitated. Patsy Cline finished her ode to lost love, and the quarters in the juke-box ran out. The place was dead silent. Everyone was looking at me and the kid, the three girls, Sam, and even the sorry alcoholic. I stood there in my clean white T and pressed tan khakis, looking down into his deer-in-a-headlight blue eyes.

Maybe he was scared, maybe he was confused, but he found enough bravado to mutter "Fuck you." Just not enough to say it real loud or look me in the eye when he said it. He crossed his arms across his belly and pulled the cool shirt up over his head. The thick bushes of blond hair in his pits were matted with sweat.

I was deciding maybe I'd been wrong about the boy. Actually, very definitely I was wrong. He was beautiful. A farmer tan darkened his arms, face, and neck. Otherwise, except for a bright red blush, his skin was white. Nice chest, just beginning to fill out. A few blond hairs curled around his nipples, quarter-size flat pink circles that had never been worked. A challenge. He wore his green fatigues so loose that only his cantilevered ass kept them from falling down. Torso damp with sweat. Nice smell. Nice boy.

Maybe he was just a kid, but he had potential, and I was already starting to make plans. I wanted more than the shirt.

The kid stood there looking at the floor. The blush had spread from his cheeks along his neck and all the way down to the upper curve of his lily-white chest. He swept the two 20s off the bar and loped out through the front door, his gangly long arms swinging wildly at his side. The three girls stared open-mouthed. Something for them to take back to sociology 101. Big fucking deal.

The bar was so quiet you could here the faucet dripping into the sink under Sam's bar. Someone put another quarter in the jukebox. "Tennessee Waltz." I left a $10 bill on the bar and walked out into the parking lot.

The kid was standing in the middle of the lot, his damp torso gleaming in the sodium vapor light. He was shivering. It gets cold fast up in the foothills once the sun goes down. It was a clear, starry night, inky black outside the circle of light in the parking lot.

I walked up to the kid, stripped off my white T, and handed it to him. I stood bare-chested just long enough for him to get a look at me, my flat belly and defined pecs covered with swirls of black hair. Then I pulled on the shirt. It slipped on snugly over my shoulders. The words *power back* stretched out over my pecs. I was right about the shirt. It fit me just fine.

"See, kid. I told you. Cool shirt."

The kid swallowed and looked down at the ground. He didn't seem to be going anywhere. He didn't pull on the white T-shirt. His back was to the service alley along the side of the bar. I put my hands on his bare shoulders and pushed him backward into the darkness.

The air smelled of stale beer and piss combined with the mix of chaparral and pine in the crisp mountain air. I laid my body into him, pushing his back against the rough unpainted stucco. I ran my hands from his shoulders along his flanks, slipping under the waistband of his jockey shorts until my palms rested on his hip bones. Ridges of firm muscle under a thin layer of baby fat. Nice.

I slid my hands around his ass until my fingers found the moist, hairy crack of his ass cheeks, then back out and up to his tits, two tender spots on his firm flat pecs.

Nipples that had never been worked over. I rubbed them a little with the workout calluses on the palms of my hands, then pincered them with two fingers and the thumb of each hand. Gentle at first, then harder. I kept my eyes on his face. His expression isn't easy to describe. More amazed, I guess, than anything else. He looked into my eyes for a while, then down, watching my hands working his nipples.

When I thought he was ready, I dug in, hard enough for him to really feel the bite of my nails. The kid opened his mouth to gasp, and I leaned down and kissed him on the mouth. I guessed it was his first kiss from a man. He tried to clamp his mouth shut, but I dug into his tits a little harder, and he opened wide. I ground the stubble of my beard into his face, a real man's kiss, big, wet, and beery-mouthed.

My cock was starting to stretch itself down the left leg of my khakis. I could feel the kid getting excited too. His cock and balls all bunched up in the pouch of his briefs. The weight of my body kept him pressed against the wall. I probed his mouth with my tongue. He gave up. He was taking my tongue now, sucking it deeper into his mouth.

Nice mouth. I bent my knees a bit and pressed my crotch into his. He was already hard. Real hard.

I pulled my face away for a second and looked into his eyes, keeping up the pressure on his crotch. "You want it, kid. I know you do," I said.

He looked down to where our hips were pressed together and shook his head. But the no didn't mean shit.

I slipped my hand into his briefs and straightened out the kink in his cock. The least I could do. Nice cock, thick and long, like a boy's should be. Nice cock, but I'd have to save it for later. Now it was time for the kid to get to work. Gripping him firmly by the shoulders, I forced him onto his knees, scraping his bare back on the stucco on the way down.

I teased him for a minute while I undid my belt and let my pants drop down to my knees. My cock looped out, half-hard and thick, just an inch from the kid's wide-eyed face. He looked up at me, half-afraid, half begging. Like a puppy for a bone.

I'm pretty big, so I didn't want to give him too long to think. I pried open his mouth with my thumb and forefinger and slid myself in to the back of his throat. Now was the time; as I got harder I was pretty sure the kid wouldn't be able to take it all the way. Not many men could.

But the kid did just fine. As hard as my cock got, it didn't matter. Gagging, drooling from his mouth and nose, almost puking, that buzzcut blond head kept on bobbing, that sweet mouth kept on sucking, and I kept on fucking. Fucking that kid's beautiful face. That soft virgin mouth.

When I got close I slowed down. A couple of long, smooth strokes. Out. Cock head bobbing in front of his open, begging mouth until the kid gave in and just dived for it, openmouthed. Good puppy. Back in. All the way home to the bruised flesh at the back of his throat. I wanted him to feel me. To feel the first load of man come as it filled his mouth and throat. Hot come burning out of his nostrils.

When I couldn't hold it back anymore, I grabbed his ears and pulled him forward, buried his face in my crotch. And came.

He suckled for a minute while my cock softened in his mouth. A nice feeling, a man sucking out the last of your come. After a minute or two I pulled him off and lifted him to his feet. His swollen cock head still poked out above the waistband of his jeans. And his belly glistened with come. No hands. Good boy.

I picked the white T up from where he had dropped it on the cement. I helped him put it on. He was shaking.

I put my arm around his shoulder and pulled him up against my chest. "It's OK, boy," I said. "When do you have to get back to base?"

"I'm on leave," he answered. "I ran out of money, so I was heading back early."

"How about coming back to my place and we'll talk things over?" He swallowed and looked up at me, looking for reassurance that it was OK. I smiled and walked over to my pickup and opened the passenger door, then walked over to my side and got behind the wheel. By the time I started up the engine, he had climbed in and was sitting in the passenger seat, his lean shoulders shaking in the cold.

Cool shirt.

Cool kid.

Ryan Field

*W*hen I was a senior in college, I started hanging around a straight nightclub called Vibrations. I had just broken up with my first lover, a football player who left me for a cheerleader because he decided he wasn't gay (he just liked the way I sucked dick). Even though I knew I was gay, I wasn't ready for the gay bars yet. All I wanted to do was wallow in my own misery.

I blended well in the straight bar. I've always had that all-American look: blond hair, blue eyes, and a strong chin. No one ever knows I'm gay unless I tell them. At that time in my life, I wanted to hide in a place that felt safe. Club Vibrations was my comfort zone.

At 21 years old I was still jacking off about three times a day. Despite my depressed state, or perhaps because of it, I needed to release all the fluids from my body. I'd pull into the parking lot at Vibrations, whack myself off, lick up all the come, and then go inside to watch the boys and girls have fun. I always went directly to a bar on the lower level of the club and perched on a corner stool where I could become invisible.

It's funny how uninhibited straight women can be if they are interested in a man—so unlike the games gay men play with each other. At least twice an evening a young lady would approach me, asking if I wanted another beer or if I wanted to dance with her. I always declined, politely saying, "I'm sorry but thank you. I'm only out for a couple of beers. I'm engaged to be married." It was a lie, but it was kind, and the women always appreciated the fact that I didn't cheat on my girlfriend.

Vibrations became a haven for me, to the point where I knew all the people at the front door and my favorite bartender knew exactly what I was going to order. Sometimes I didn't even have to sit down and my drink was already waiting for me. Most times I didn't even have to pay, which actually cost me more in the long run because I'd wind up leaving a really big tip.

My favorite bartender also happened to be extremely hot looking. He was tall, with a short dark blond military haircut and dark blue eyes. He always wore plaid shirts, Levi's, and work boots. I knew we worked out at the same gym, but I'd never seen him there because we both had different hours. And although I had a nicely defined body, he obviously worked out more often. It was nice to admire his great ass and the way his dick touched the tops of the alcohol bottles when he leaned over the bar. I didn't drool, and I wasn't obvious, but I couldn't help thinking he'd be a great top man.

Then one night he said, "Hey, buddy, you've been coming here for a while now and I don't know your name." "It's Ryan," I told him.

"I'm Joe," he said with a smile, showing me the dimples in his cheeks. Then he extended me a handshake.

I was certainly taken aback. I'd been to my share of bars, straight and gay, and no bartender ever introduced himself to me—at least not formally.

For the rest of the evening he kept coming back, between customers, and talking. It turned out we had a great deal in common. He rented a cabinet in an antiques co-op, and I worked part-time for an antiques dealer.

"How'd you like to grab a bite to eat when this joint closes down later?" he asked me after the DJ announced the last call.

"Um, well, I guess so," I told him apprehensively. I hadn't eaten at all that day, but there was a coffee cake back at the dorms I'd been saving for that night's binge.

"Great," he said. "Wait for me outside in the parking lot. I've got a big black pickup truck parked near the back door."

"OK," I said, " I'll meet you there."

While I was outside waiting, I was kicking myself for saying yes. Why in the world would I want to get friendly with a straight bartender? He'd probably bring a couple of girls out with him and then I'd be stuck for the rest of the night. I actually thought about just going home, but I realized I'd never be able to go to that bar again. I couldn't leave a note; I didn't have a pen and paper. Just as I was imagining the worst that could happen, I saw him walking toward the truck. All by himself.

"So where do you want to go?" he asked.

"Anywhere you want," I said quietly. I'm normally not shy, unless I'm in a situation where I feel cornered.

"I know this great place called Laura's about 20 minutes from here. It's got great food and it's not like a greasy diner."

"OK," I said, now thinking to myself that this was going to be a long, long evening, "I'll follow you."

"Why don't you just drop your car off at my place? I live just a few minutes from here. I hate to drive in tandem."

"OK," I said, kicking myself. Now I was stuck with him.

Thankfully, the ride to Laura's went quickly. We both had so much in common that once the conversation got going the time just flew by. Before I even realized it, three hours had passed and we were back in his driveway saying good night.

"You OK to drive, buddy?" he asked, concerned about my getting home.

"Sure," I told him. "It's not that far."

"You want to get together tomorrow night and watch the game with me? We'll get a couple of pizzas or something."

"OK," I said, kicking myself again. The last thing I wanted to do was watch a baseball game with a straight guy. And what if he invited more of his straight friends?

"C'mon over anytime after 5," he told me.

"Great," I said. "So long."

"See you tomorrow, buddy," he said. "Be careful."

On the way home I told myself that starting next week I was going to go to gay bars again. There was nothing wrong with hanging out with a straight guy, but I also needed to be with my own kind too. This wasn't normal.

The next evening I showed up at his front door with a six-pack of beer and a bag of chips. I wanted to bring a bottle of white wine and a basket of muffins but I thought that might be too gay.

"C'mon in, buddy," he said." Make yourself at home."

I was in shock. The apartment was well-decorated with a combination of antiques and reproductions. And it was spotlessly clean. I had imagined plaid sofas, secondhand end tables, and sweat socks rolled up in the corners.

I sat on a large comfortable sectional sofa while he poured me a beer. He poured himself a glass of white wine.

"You want to go down to the pool for a swim before the game starts?" he asked.

"I don't have a suit."

"Then you'll have to swim in your underwear."

I must have looked stunned because he quickly said, "I have one you can borrow." He laughed to himself as he went into the bedroom.

When he returned he was wearing a red string bikini. I didn't want to stare, but I couldn't help notice that he had a basket between his legs that looked like a sack of potatoes.

"Here," he said, handing me a black bikini, "go put this on."

Again, the entire time we were at the pool we talked and laughed two hours away. I was actually enjoying myself; this new friendship might be the best thing in the world for me.

When we were back in the apartment he said, "You mind if we just watch the game in our underwear? I don't feel like getting dressed."

"I don't mind," I said, with chagrin, "but I don't have any. I mean, I don't usually wear underwear."

He smiled and said, "I'll loan you a pair of those too." He went into the bedroom and I shouted, "Boxers if you have them." I was afraid I'd get hard in front of him.

A pair of plaid boxer shorts and a white towel came flying out the door.

"Thanks," I yelled and then quickly yanked myself out of the bathing suit and into the boxers. I kept trying to think about non-sexual things to remain flaccid.

"You want to order pizza now or later?" he asked, returning to the room wearing a pair of short white boxers.

"Later," I said, walking over to the bar for another beer.

Hell, I was beginning to enjoy this. I could drink all the beer I wanted and not worry. This was a straight guy. So what if my stomach blew up like a balloon? He wouldn't give a shit.

He was already seated on the sofa when I returned, propped directly in the center, leaving me the choice of either end. I chose the right side.

We weren't on the sofa more than two minutes when he reached over and ran his large hand along my upper thigh.

"Damn, buddy," he said, "you got smooth legs. I was watching by the pool. Do you shave them?"

"About twice a month I use a hair-removing cream all over my body. It lets me see if I'm getting results from my workouts. Besides, I'm not all that hairy to begin with. Plus, I jog at the park and I can see if there are any ticks on me if I don't have hair. I don't want Lyme disease."

"Well, it looks good," he said. "Stand up."

"What?" I asked.

"Stand up, buddy."

I wasn't hard when I stood up. I was too amazed at what was happening.

He ran his hand up my thigh, into the boxer shorts, and cupped half my ass with his large hand.

"Joe, what are you doing?" I asked.

"Should I stop?"

I stared into his blue eyes and did not respond. He pulled his hand out of my shorts, stood up, and bent me over the back of the sofa. I did not protest.

"Can I take off your shorts?" he asked.

"OK," I told him, holding my dick so that the shorts would slide down easily.

"Damn!" he shouted. "Spread those pretty legs as far as you can and arch your back. That's the sweetest thing I've ever seen. What a great fucking pussy, *baby!*"

I did as I was told while he stood and admired me.

"Can we do one little kinky thing?" he asked.

"What?"

"Will you please put these on? Please, for me." He pulled a pair of black high heels out from under the sofa. Six-inch heels. Then he pulled out a garter belt and a pair of black fishnet stockings.

"I don't know, Joe," I told him. "I never did drag. I'm not into that sort of thing."

"But it's not drag. You're not wearing makeup or anything else. It's just a small fetish of mine. Just the high heels and stockings. Please. Pretty please," he begged.

Without saying yes, I grabbed the kink and went into the bedroom. I figured that if this was what he liked, it would be better to put them on somewhere else and then enter the room.

I was right. When I came back in, wearing nothing but a garter belt, fishnets, and heels, Joe nearly lost his mind. "Baby, come sit on my lap," he said.

This was the most unusual thing I'd ever done. Hell, I was still shocked that Joe put the moves on me. I must also admit, having him so excited about the heels and stockings was very stimulating. If I felt foolish when I entered the room, I was melting like butter when I sat on his lap and heard him moan with pure delight.

"You know," he said, licking my shoulder, "I don't do this often. I mean, it's not often I find a guy like you who I feel comfortable enough with to ask him to wear this stuff. And it's not often anyone looks so damn sexy in them."

Then he lifted me up and placed me over the back of the sofa again.

"Spread those legs," he ordered.

I did as I was told and arched my back as much as I could. I only wanted to please this man.

He started to lick the shoes and suck the heels. Then he ran his wet tongue over every inch of my fishnet-covered legs. He was working his way up to the center of my ass.

I moaned and he asked, "Do you like that, baby? You want me to rub my rough beard on that sweet ass?"

"Oh, yes. Yes," I begged. It wasn't as if I was the submissive and he was the dominant. We were both trying to please each other.

"Turn around," he told me. "I want to see that pretty face."

Gently, he grabbed me by the waist and helped me ease around and sit on the sofa. Then he lifted my legs in the air and threw them over his shoulders, pressing his entire body into mine. I was pinned, scrunched up against the sofa with my legs in the air, high heels dangling down his back.

"I want to taste those lips," he said.

Then he pressed his lips against mine. First it was easy and soft. Then he shoved his tongue down my throat. I wanted to swallow it, that's how great it tasted. I sucked it and licked it and ran my own tongue over every tooth in his mouth.

With his strong hands he cupped my pecs. He squeezed them and massaged them and pinched the nipples.

"You got a great chest, baby, real worked out. I could suck on those tits all day long." He must have sucked my nipples for nearly 20 minutes. I moaned and groaned to the point where I thought I might come just from having him play with my tits.

"Wrap your legs around my waist and your arms around my neck," he whispered, "I'm going to carry you to the bed."

I did as I was told, and he lifted me up from the sofa. His strong hands were pressed against my ass, holding me in place.

"Mind if I put on a pair of Army boots?" he asked.

"No," I said. He still hadn't removed his white boxer shorts, and I could see a huge hard cock begging to break loose. I didn't say anything though. Maybe he liked it that way.

I noticed a tube of red lipstick on the nightstand by the bed. I knew what that was for. Without even asking, I leaned over and started to put on the red lipstick.

"I was hoping you'd find that," he said, lacing up his black Army boots.

"Please," I joked, "you knew I'd see it."

"Well, I didn't have to force you to put it on," he teased.

"You don't have to force me to do anything, big boy," I told him.

"Prove it," he said, standing over me at the foot of the bed. He spread his legs and yanked his dick out of the fly in his shorts. It was huge and thick.

As I got down on all fours and crawled toward him like a cat, I caught a glimpse of myself in the mirror. I looked fucking hot! Anywhere else I would have looked like a freak. But in bed with him, doing this, I looked fucking sexy!

"Damn, that looks good enough to eat," I said, cupping his large balls with one hand and his big cock with the other. I stuck my tongue out and started to lick.

First I started to lick up his precome. I milked his cock until a large drop formed at the opening, then I lapped it up with the tip of my tongue and swallowed it like candy. He moaned with delight.

"Wrap those pretty red lips around that big dick," he said. "Let me see you slide them up and down the whole shaft."

I took the whole dick like a pro cocksucker. It tasted like gold too. I sucked until my jaws hurt. And then I sucked some more. I only wanted to hear him moan with pleasure, which he did, time and again.

"You like to suck cock?" he asked.

"Not usually," I told him truthfully, "but I do like to suck this one."

He tilted his head for a moment, knowing that I was telling him the truth. I think his cock grew another half inch after I said that.

"Do you want to come?" I asked him, ready to swallow his entire load.

"Oh, yes," he said, "but not like this."

"How?" I asked, only too happy to please him.

"Go over there and lie on your back," he said, pointing to a workout bench.

As I stood he told me, "Shake that ass while you walk. I want to watch it move."

I did as I was told. He whistled and said, "Yes, baby. That's one great ass! I'm gonna plow it like a maniac."

When I was on my back I figured I'd throw my legs over the barbell.

"That's right," he said. "I didn't even have to tell you to do that. You know you're gonna get your brains fucked out."

He walked over to me, squatted down, and started to lick my ass. I moaned and pinched my nipples while his tongue went in and out of my desperate hole.

"Damn, that tastes good," Joe said. "I don't suck cock, but I sure do love to eat a pretty hole like this."

"You don't have to suck cock," I told him. "This is better for me."

He ate my hole for a long time. Then he started to work his finger inside. I kept moaning and groaning, and my dick was standing like a flagpole.

"Can I fuck that pussy, baby?" he asked.

"I think so," I told him. "I mean, I really want you to."

"I'm gonna use a condom and some lube just to be on the safe side. I know I'm not positive, and you probably aren't. But it's better to be safe than sorry."

"I'm negative," I told him. "I swear to God. And I don't sleep around. This is the first time I've ever really done this."

"You're a virgin?" he asked.

"Never done it before," I told him.

"Well, holy shit," he said. "I never had a virgin! That means that your ass will always belong to me. You know that."

"I never thought of it that way," I told him.

"That's right," he said. "That pretty hole is mine!" And then he opened his mouth and jammed it into my hole.

It felt like I was going to have an out-of-body experience. The way his beard rubbed against my skin, how his tongue explored my hole.

I guess he trusted me completely because the next thing he did was spread a glob of jelly all around my hole. Then, with two fingers, he went inside and spread some jelly in there too. Then he started to fuck me with his two fingers, telling me, "I just want to get that little virgin hole ready."

It hurt a little at first. But as he continued to fuck me with his fingers in a slow, steady rhythm, it started to feel wonderful.

"You like to get finger-fucked, don't you?"

"Oh, yes," I said. "Don't stop."

He continued fucking for a few more minutes and then said, "Get up and go outside on the balcony. Lean over the rail and spread those pretty legs for me."

I looked outside. There was a French door in the bedroom that lead to a small balcony.

"Don't worry," he told me. "It's private."

He helped me lower my legs from the barbell, and I slowly walked out of the room. I knew his eyes were staring at my ass the entire time.

When I was outside I leaned over the fence that surrounded the balcony and spread my legs for him. He mounted me in seconds, shoving his cock into my hole hard and fast. At first it was pain like I'd never known. But he simply stood there with his rock-hard dick inside me and said, "I know it hurt. But just wait a minute. You'll like it. I promise."

After a minute, when the initial pain subsided, he started to fuck slowly and evenly, just in and out. My own erection had gone down for a minute, but I was hard as a rock again in no time.

"That's it, baby," he said, fucking harder. "Nice and tight. Squeeze my big fat dick with that pretty pussy."

His hands were wrapped around my hips, fucking me with a beat that was making me wild.

"I'm close," I told him.

"But you haven't even touched your dick," he said.

"I don't have to," I said. "You're making me come just by fucking me this way."

"Good boy," he said, "I'm going to fill that pretty pussy. It's gonna shoot so far you'll feel it in your stomach. Fuck, baby, what a sweet ass!"

"Oh, yes, Joey," I said. "Fuck me harder. Ram my fucking pussy as hard as you can. Go real deep. Hold my ass tightly. Then pull that big cock out and ram it again."

I had never been so uninhibited before. With the football player there was no dialogue. He came to my room, opened his fly, and I sucked him off. After I licked him clean he'd shove his cock back into his pants and leave me alone. Sometimes he said "Thank you," but most of the time he was silent.

With Joey it was different. We were screaming filth to each other, but it wasn't dirty. It was magnificent. He knew how much I loved getting my hole filled with his big dick, but he didn't treat me like a piece of garbage. The entire experience was like trying on a familiar old glove.

Joey went deep and than slid his cock out, and then he went deep again. It was a constant motion. My legs were spread so far apart it's a wonder I didn't fall off the six-inch heels. Finally I couldn't take it anymore. I had to come.

He knew without even being told, and he started to ram me faster and harder until I screamed, "Yes, Joey, yes! Harder! Faster!"

"I'm gonna shoot too, baby," he said, "I'm gonna fill that pussy till it drips."

The fucking motion was fast and hard, and we both shot our loads at the same time. I must have shot a bucket of juice, and I never touched my dick once. I knew he was coming too. His hands started to squeeze me ass cheeks harder, and I could feel the head of his dick swelling inside my pussy.

The moment after he came he shoved his dick into my hole as deeply as he could. It was as if we were welded together.

"Stand up straight," he told me, "and we'll walk back to the bed like this."

We fell onto the bed, and he remained inside me. I tried to spread my legs as far as I could to accommodate him. His cock was still rock-hard.

"Are you OK?" he asked.

"I want to stay like this forever," I told him.

"Can I leave my cock inside you?" he asked.

"You can do anything you want," I told him.

"Let's take a short nap just like this," he said. "We'll rest up for later."

He was whispering in my ear and fucking me gently. I started to get semi-hard again.

"What about the game?" I asked.

"Fuck the game," he said. "I'm gonna plow this sweet little hole at least three more times tonight and then I'm gonna ram it again in the morning. Remember, that's my ass now. You're gonna be wearing those high heels for the next 24 hours at least."

"If my ass is yours now," I asked, "does that mean that your big dick belongs to me?"

"Every last inch of it," he whispered as he fell asleep on top of me."

As it turned out, I wore those high heels for the next 15 years.

The Woodsman

Lee Nichols

I was standing at the sink in the kitchen staring out the window at what had once been my woodpile as a wave of regret sloshed over me. A month earlier I'd fled San Francisco to this picturesque house near the village of Albion on California's rugged north coast. For the first two weeks things had been great: The deer came to eat apples that fell from the ancient trees, the sun was still warm most of the day, and in the evenings a small fire in the wood stove in the kitchen warmed up the whole house in minutes. Best of all, my novel was progressing better than I could have hoped. It got a little lonely three miles up the narrow road from the village, but, hell, being lonely was better than living with my drugged-out ex-boyfriend in a flat I couldn't really afford on what the PR firm I worked for paid me to write copy about computer companies.

Then the weather turned cold—*really* cold—and I spent time I should have been writing cutting stove-size pieces out of the huge leftover hunks of redwood, pine, and oak in the dwindling woodpile. This morning I was trying to warm the house with last Sunday's *San Francisco Chronicle* and two pieces of pine I picked up on the road, sticks that had fallen off a truck some firewood guy was delivering to somebody who'd ordered it in midsummer.

It wasn't that I hadn't tried to buy wood. Christ, I'd called every firewood guy listed in the yellow rages and posted a FIRE-WOOD WANTED sign on the bulletin board at the Albion Market. I even screwed up my nerve enough to ignore the NO TRESPASSING sign and invade the privacy of my only neighbor to ask if he knew where I could get some firewood. He said the same thing everybody else had: I should have bought my wood in summer. Nobody had any wood now. And what the hell was I thinking of anyway, moving to Deer Meadow in fall without knowing where I'd get my firewood?

That was the state of affairs I contemplated as I stared at the six or eight pieces of wood left, pieces too big for the stove and too hard to yield to my Boy Scout ax or dull ripsaw. Then Thomas arrived.

I heard the truck before I saw it; a big red truck loaded with firewood, backing into the drive through the open gate, maneuvering toward the empty woodpile. It stopped and the driver hopped out. I stared. Then I wiped my hand across my eyes—I really did—to test whether the vision I'd seen was a hallucination. When I looked again he was still there—and still a vision. He stretched like a kitten and slowly pulled on a pair of gloves, making his hands the most fully covered part of his body. His

chest was bare. His legs were bare. His butt and groin were barely concealed by the shortest, most tattered pair of cutoff Levi's
I'd ever seen. And to add to my fantasy, he was built like a gym-
nast. I've always had a thing for gymnasts.

The waking dream boy began tossing firewood from his truck
onto my woodpile. I adjusted myself and headed out to talk to
him. "You the fellow who delivers firewood?" I asked stupidly.
Under the circumstances, being able to talk at all was nothing
short of amazing since as I got close I'd discovered he was also
movie-actor handsome. He had a cleft chin, an easy smile that
crinkled around his baby-blue eyes, and a buzzcut that showed
off his perfectly shaped head.

"You're nearly out," he said.

"Yeah. Do you deliver here regularly?"

"First time. I saw you needed wood. I had a load. No sense in
taking it all the way to town when you need it here." He went
back to tossing pitchy pine, hunks of redwood, and sticks of
chinquapin on the pile.

It finally occurred to me to ask how much he was charging,
not that I was about to tell him to load it back on his truck no
matter how much be was charging. "Sixty," he said. That was
cheaper than what firewood people would have charged if they'd
had any wood to sell.

"You take a check?" I asked.

"Will they cash it at the Albion store?" he asked. I assured him
they would, he nodded, and I went in the house, took a deep
breath, and gave myself a lecture about not coming on to
strangers. I found my checkbook, and then I stood at the window
watching him, eating him with my gaze, ravishing him in my daydream. As he climbed up on his truck to retrieve the last few
sticks, I wandered back out. His evenly tanned torso was glistening with sweat, and even his cutoffs were soaked.

"Who do I make the check to?" I asked.

"Thomas Scofield," be said, smiling down at me.

I filled in his name and handed the check up to him. He leaned down to take it.

The leg of his cut-offs gapped. He was not wearing underwear. I turned as red as his truck and looked away. I thought I heard him chuckle.

"You got any beer?" he asked as I studied the ground at my feet.

"Sure, I'll get it."

"I'll come in when I finish," he said, jumping off the truck. "Maybe I could wash up too?"

I had a vision of Thomas asking to take a shower, leaving the bathroom door open, calling me to come bring him a towel, or maybe to wash his back. None of which happened. He washed his face at the kitchen sink, wiped it with a T-shirt he had brought in, accepted a beer, and we sat on the rear deck.

Over the next hour he told me about his life, all 27 years of it, and about all the women in it, including the one he was currently living with. Then he asked about my life and seemed genuinely interested to hear that I was a writer. I guess that was when I mentioned that I was going to Australia on assignment for a travel magazine in two weeks. Thomas volunteered to house-sit while I was away. I agreed, we shook hands on it, and he left.

Two weeks later Thomas showed up just as I was pulling out of the drive with only just enough time to get to San Francisco to catch my flight. I handed him the house key and told him to eat anything he found in the fridge or the cupboard. It wasn't till I was sitting in the Qantas terminal that it occurred to me that I hadn't de-queered the house. There were copies of *The Advocate* in the basket by the john, the poster of a half-naked cowboy was pinned to the wall by my bed, and in the drawer of the nightstand were three one-hand books and a jar of lube. I consoled myself with the thought that I'd have come out to him sometime, and leaving that stuff around was probably an easy way to do it.

I didn't think of the implication of my oversight again till I returned 20 days later. When I pulled into the driveway, there was a welcoming plume of smoke rising from the chimney. Thomas' truck was parked close to the front deck, and a strange dog was wagging its body and tail as it approached. Thomas stepped onto the porch and called to the dog. Then he came to the car and carried my bags inside. "There's coffee. I made it fresh," he said, holding the door for me.

He poured us each a cup of coffee, and we sat at the kitchen table. "Everything go OK?" I asked.

"Fine," he said, not making eye contact.

I hesitated for a beat or two. When it was clear he wasn't going to say anything more, I decided to clear the air. "You know I'm gay."

He nodded. "I accidentally looked in the drawer by your bed," he said quietly.

"Right," I said, drawing a deep breath. "So—?"

"It's OK with me. I mean, it's none of my business. I'm not. Not at all. But I had a friend once in school who was—"

"What's the dog's name?" I interrupted, having heard that story from "sympathetic" straight men once too many times already.

"Schuyler," he said, glad to have the topic changed.

Silence descended again. Finally Thomas cleared his throat. "The room in the barn? The one that looks like somebody used it for a bedroom?"

"Yeah?"

"I was wondering… You remember the lady I told you about? The one I was living with?"

"Yes?"

"She's got somebody else. While I was staying here she said she got lonesome and had a guy move in with her."

I nodded. "So you've got no place to stay?"

"Right," he said, looking at the floor.

"You're welcome to the room in the barn."

He spent a couple of days fixing up his room and then returned to his woodsman's routine: gone before I got up and rarely home before dark. I invited him to have dinner several times, and after he finally accepted we ate together nearly every night. On December 18 he came home with a six-foot pine he'd cut on timber company land. He made a stand for it, and the next day I drove into Fort Bragg and bought decorations at Thrifty. While I was in town I stopped at Reynolds' men's store and bought Thomas a heavy wool shirt and pair of Levi's, which Mrs. Reynolds wrapped for me. I put them under the tree. The next day there was a small store-wrapped package under the tree with my name on it.

On the 24th we had turkey and trimmings and managed to drink a bottle and a half of a pretty good wine I'd picked up at Harvest Market. Thomas insisted on doing the dishes, so I went back to work for an hour. Then we went to the living room and Thomas opened his gifts. To my surprise, the package with my name on it was nowhere to be seen.

We watched some TV, and at about 10 I called it a night, wished Thomas a "Merry Christmas," and went to my room, still puzzled about the gift he didn't give me. It must have been about 15 minutes later when he knocked at my door. "You asleep?" he asked softly.

"Nearly," I said.

He pushed open the door and stepped into my room. He was not wearing a shirt. "I thought I'd take a shower," he said, looking at me strangely.

"Sure."

"And then—like—give you your present."

"OK."

"Don't go to sleep. I'll shower fast."

"OK."

"Promise you won't go to sleep," he said earnestly.

"I promise," I said.

He grinned. Then his hand went to his crotch and he took hold of his cock. "I won't be long."

It seemed to me he was taking the longest shower in the history of showers. Finally I heard the water stop running. A few minutes later he came into the room and turned on the light. He had a towel around his waist.

"The light's really bright," he said switching it off. "OK if I get the candles from the living room?" He didn't wait for permission. A couple of moments later he was back with the candles. He put one on my dresser and one on the nightstand. The room glowed with the yellow light. He sat on the edge of the bed. I could smell the fresh scent of him, fell the warmth of him. He reached down and took my hand and slowly brought it to his chest and pressed my palm against his pectoral. I ran my finger across his nipple. He sighed and shifted position so that he was half lying beside me.

I moved my hand down his chest slowly, stopping at his navel to run my finger round it and in and out. He laughed. I moved my hand down till I felt the top of the towel. Thomas reached down and pulled the towel off. I inched my hand lower—lower—till I felt the hair, the base of his shaft. He was hard. I wrapped my fingers around it, and he shifted again, lying against me now, my hand between us. Then I felt his hand on my stomach. I arched my back to give him access. He slipped his hand into my briefs, touched the tip of my cock with one finger, and ran his finger across the head spreading the precome over it.

"I checked your medicine cabinet," he whispered.

"Why?"

"You don't take anything. No pills. You must not have—you know."

"I don't. I'm negative."

"Me too." Then he laughed. "Unless I got it from my old lady."

I managed to slip down so that I could take him in my mouth. He groaned contentedly and moved his cock slowly in and out while I massaged the back of his shaft with my tongue and his balls with my hand. "Have you ever done this before—with a man?"

"No. Never knew anybody who'd want to," he said as he twisted on the bed till his mouth was at my crotch. "Tell me if I'm not doing it right," he said as he took me deep into his mouth.

I would have warned him if there'd been time, but a couple of seconds after he started sucking I came—explosively, torrentially, wildly. To my surprise, he didn't pull away. "Sorry," I finally mumbled. "I should have warned you."

"Coming's the whole idea, isn't it?" he said, wiping his mouth with the back of his hand. "Would it be OK if we took a breather? I'd like a beer before you take care of me."

Thomas stoked the fire, fixed me a scotch, got himself a beer, and we sat side by side at the kitchen table, naked, his hand on my leg, mine in his lap, fingers encircling his flaccid penis. "I don't know how this happened, but it's the best Christmas present I've had ever," I said.

"Since the first day when you were taking my clothes off with your eyes, I've been thinking, *Why the fuck not?* I mean, coming's coming, right? When you have sex with somebody you like, it's better. I like you, you want to have sex with me, so why the fuck not?" He slugged down the last of his beer. "Only I haven't come yet." He pulled me to my feet. "After you suck me off I want to talk about getting fucked. I've always wondered what it would be like. That's what I had wrapped up for you under the tree, a bunch of rubbers. But I guess we don't have to use 'em, right?"

"Still a good idea."

"I guess. Hell, it won't make any difference to the way it feels to me I guess."

He came in my mouth, which seemed only fair. We had a cigarette. He unwrapped a condom and rolled it on me, we lubed, and I fucked him for a while. It was hard to believe it was the first time for him, but after a couple of minutes he shifted position and I pulled out. "I like sucking better," he announced, pulling the condom off and going down on me.

By dawn I'd had four orgasms and Thomas had had five. We slept until 1 on Christmas day. I fixed breakfast, Thomas put on his new shirt, and we drove to Navarro Beach to let Schuyler chase gulls. As we were getting back into his truck, Thomas laid his hand on mine. "I still like ladies more. I mean, I miss the teats. I'm a teat man; always have been."

I nodded. "Even if we never do it again, I have to tell you, it was the best sex I've ever had."

"Who said we won't?" he asked, starting the engine. "What else have we got to do? It's Christmas, man. A day to enjoy ourselves."

Finally Friday

Edgar Wayne

*I*t's amazing what life blinds us to. Here I was living a life that didn't make sense, moving day to day in a haze. Until my junior year in college, I had denied who I was. But the years caught up with me, and I was about to explode from all the emotion and desire I had built up inside. It was the moment my life changed forever—and for the better.

I had finally acknowledged that I was gay and started trying to meet people. On my fourth trip to a local bar, after sitting by myself the previous trips, I met the most gorgeous man I had ever seen. In fact, to this day, I have not met anyone who can even compare. I was sitting alone when I noticed a group of guys sitting in front of me, and one was staring at me. I stared back, and this went on for what seemed like hours. No matter where I went in the bar, his eyes never left me. Even when he went onto the dance floor with someone else, I caught him throwing glances—glances I felt the need to return. Inexperienced as I was, I was trying to figure out how to connect with him, when—

"What time do you have?"

As I looked up from my watch, I thought I was going to die. I was in complete shock as I answered, "It's just before 2." This gorgeous man standing over me, and here I was, this novice, feeling like a boy in a man's world.

"So does this club stay open late for dancing, or does it clear out?"

"They're open till 4," I managed to say. "It doesn't seem like this place ever clears out." My heart was pounding, my palms were sweating, and all I kept thinking was that this couldn't be happening

I waited for him to say something else. He didn't. The next thing I knew he smiled and walked over to the bar. I decided I better just look away. But before I knew it I had this weird yet wonderful feeling. It was like someone was standing behind me. I don't mean even a foot behind me. I could feel the person's body up against mine as I sat on my bar stool. I waited for about a minute and slowly turned to see him standing there grinning. He tilted his head to one side, flashed the largest smile I've ever seen, and walked back over to his group of friends.

I knew I wasn't prepared to deal with this. So I figured I would hit, then run like hell. With that brilliant idea, I slowly worked my way toward him.

"Hi, my name's Eddie."

"I'm Marc." He flashed that smile again. "I was hoping you would come over."

"Well, actually I'm on my way out. But I was wondering if you would like to meet for drinks later in the week—"

"Definitely." He reached over and put his hand on my shoulder. "To be honest, I'd like to get together tonight, but I'll wait."

"Well, this has been a bad week, and things should ease up by Friday." With this, I put my hand on his back, leaned toward him to speak in his ear, and told him I was looking forward to Friday. I was looking forward to it more than he would ever know. As I left, his eyes never once left me.

On my way home I kept trying to reassure myself that this had actually happened. Here I was, this shy, somewhat bookwormish young man, and I was going to be meeting the man of my dreams for drinks in six days; the longest six days that I would ever experience.

Finally, Friday arrived and so did I, at the bar. About five minutes later he came in. He was more beautiful than I remembered.

"I was worried you wouldn't come," he said. "But I tried to put those thoughts out of my mind." Again, there was that smile.

"Really? And here I was worried that I would find myself sitting here alone come closing."

It was amazing. I had never met someone with whom I had so much in common. Perhaps that's why I was willing to do what my mother always told me not to: Before I knew it we wound up at his place. It was strange in the sense that here I was in the house of a virtual stranger, yet I felt more comfortable there than almost any other place.

"Would you like something to drink? I've got soda, but if you want, I can go out for beer."

"Soda's great."

He motioned for me to sit on the sofa. A minute later, he came in with the drinks, and we just sat and talked. Before long we were on the floor. My head was resting in his lap as he gently caressed my hair. I knew this was right. I thought that surely he would make some type of move, but, strangely enough, it never came. So I decided to make a move of my own. Even as the words *May I kiss you?* came from my lips, I couldn't believe what I was saying. I wasn't known for my assertiveness.

"I would like that."

Our first kiss was beautiful. And for me it was truly my "first kiss." It was so soft and loving. I had never experienced anything like this, and my mind was racing a thousand miles an hour. One kiss lead to another and then another. Then those kisses lead to what I had waited for all of my life. We got up, and he took my hand. He looked into my eyes and didn't say a word. Then he walked me into the bedroom.

Sitting on the edge of his bed, I will never forget what he looked like. With his short dark hair and chiseled jaw, he was like some god come to life. In addition to that beautiful smile, his blue eyes were stunning. I was more than ready to take the plunge.

He walked over toward the dresser and got something out of the drawer. As he walked back toward the bed, I could see that he was carrying a box of condoms and placed them next to me. With that, I reached up and put my hands on his shoulders. As he leaned forward to kiss me, I began to unbutton his shirt. I pushed it off his shoulders and started caressing his chest. Slowly, I worked my way down to his pants. As they slipped down around his knees, I came face-to-face with the most beautiful piece of flesh I had ever seen. Before I knew it I had my mouth full of him. As I tongued and sucked I could feel his cock get harder. It was so long and thick that I thought I wouldn't be able to take it in, but somehow I managed. As I continued I started kneading his ass with my hands, at times pulling him farther into my mouth. When my fingers reached into the crevice of his ass, he squeezed tight and moaned. Suddenly, he pulled out his throbbing cock and his come poured out onto my face.

After a little cleaning up he started to undress me. I could never explain the feeling of his hands on my body—firm yet the softest feeling I ever known. He had me on the bed and began to feast on my hard cock. As he tried to suck the come out of me, he fondled my aching balls. I gripped the sheets, and I shot off streams of come like never before. And there again was that smile.

"Fuck me!" I said and grabbed him by the waist and pulled him tight against me.

"Are you sure this is what you want?"

"Oh, yeah!" And with that I spread my legs and waited for him to thrust his cock inside me.

"Don't worry," he said, grabbing the box of rubbers. "I'll go slow."

At that point I didn't care if he went slow or fast; I just wanted him inside me.

He reached over next to the bed and got some lube and worked his finger inside me. God, it felt so good. I looked down and saw that his cock was getting harder, and he slipped on a rubber and lubed up. He held my legs up as he began to slide his tool into my tight hole.

"Oh, shit!" After that I couldn't say another word. I didn't need to, my moans said enough.

As he slowly moved farther into me, I thought I was going to split in half, but at that point I didn't care. I just wanted more. As he fucked me, I rubbed his shoulders. Then the most wonderful feeling came over me, and I began to shoot my load. Suddenly, he pulled out and ripped the condom off his bulging dick and shot his warm load across my stomach. He leaned forward, and we kissed and held each other, our hot, sticky loads strewn between our bodies.

After a couple of minutes he got up and led me to the bathroom and started a hot shower. Ever since I was young, I had had fantasies about getting it in the shower, and here was my dream come true.

"You OK? You're not saying much."

"You're my first." I tried not to look him in the eye as I said it.

"I figured. But are you OK?"

"I'm great. It was more than I could have ever expected. I want more." I thought maybe I was being too greedy, but soon we were at it again.

As the water hit our bodies, we fondled each other and got each other off. After the shower, my other longed-for wish came true.

As we went back into the bedroom, I brushed up against his back and walked him to the edge of the bed. He lay facedown in the covers as I stared to play with his firm ass. I put a rubber on my hard-on and lubed us both and then, so slowly, worked my way into him. His moans were so loud I thought the neighbors would complain. He told me he wanted to turn over to watch, so I pulled out and thrust back in as soon as he did. As my load began to fill the sheath, he grabbed his cock and started jacking off. I couldn't believe the amount of come that shot into the air, some landing on his stomach, and some shooting high enough to land on my chest.

After cleaning up again we got some sleep. Being in his arms that night was more than I could have ever wished for. Not only was the sex hot, but he also didn't expect me to walk out after he got his.

"Good morning. I hope you slept well." He kissed me and then went to the kitchen to get breakfast.

As I got up I noticed a robe at the foot of the bed. I put it on and went into the kitchen to find him pouring juice. He looked so cute in his boxers. He walked over to where I was standing and gave me a kiss. He untied my robe and slipped out of his boxers. As he turned my body around, he lifted one of my legs up onto one of the barstools and crouched down between my legs. Suddenly, I felt his tongue dancing around my hole. Slowly, he worked up into me, and I was in sheer ecstasy. When he was finished I sat up on the edge of one of the counters as he crammed the head of his dick into my hole. This was one breakfast I would never forget.

We spent the rest of the day together. That evening, when it came time to part, I had no regrets. I hated that this experience had to come to an end.

A couple of weeks later, Marc moved to California. I don't have him, but I have wonderful memories. And sometimes, when I'm alone, I think back to that wonderful night and that glorious smile, and I touch those places he made feel so right.

B.B. Wills

*A*t once we leaped out of our seats to our feet, hands out-stretched above our heads, screaming with delight to the flashing of the blue light and the whirl of the siren that signified that the good guys had scored the tying goal. This was no ordinary game. To survive this and emerge as the victors meant postseason play-off matches. As a season ticket holder I had suffered through some games but enjoyed them all. With the game tied at the end of the second period, fans and players alike needed the intermission to get themselves ready for a raucous final 20 minutes of regulation play. We continued to cheer loudly as the players made their way to the locker room.

As season ticket holders we had sat with the same neighbors all around for the entire season, and we shared the good cheer as you might with a longtime friend. I turned to my left to receive the high five that my closest neighbor offered up. The reverie subsiding, everyone, including my neighbor and I, headed for the rest room. Because of the large crowd in attendance, we ended up in line for about 10 minutes. As he struck up small talk, I became aware of how handsome he really was. He had an almost clean-shaven head and a short trimmed beard of dark, almost black, hair, eyes of brown so light they appeared to be illuminated from within, and full, luscious lips. I became mesmerized. I got to study him from behind too as I waited for a urinal to open up. Broad shoulders narrowed into a V, and two thick thighs held up a perfectly rounded piece of ass. As good fortune would have it, I stepped up to the urinal next to him as he shook a healthy Italian sausage. As he stuffed it back into his jeans, he leaned back far enough to provide me enough of a look to elicit a thickening of the meat I held in my own hand.

I made my way back to my seat to find him sitting with his legs spread wide open, blocking the aisle. As he rose, we came eye to eye, and a bolt of electricity shot between us. As the final period of play began, we settled in with our legs pressed against each other. Even though we leaped to our feet with each exciting play, our legs managed to touch each time we sat back down. The game still tied as our team began moving up the ice with less then a minute to go, the entire crowd rose to its feet in unison, alternately holding its breath and screaming as one entity. Frantic action in front of the opposition's net, a quick save by the goalie, and then at once a slap shot by one of the lesser-known rookies got the blue light flashing, the sirens wailing, and all of us screaming. Victory at last!

As we all rejoiced I expected another high five from my neighbor but was rewarded with a bear hug instead, pressing me hard against an even harder chest. Seeing the shock on my face, he must have suddenly realized what he had done and apologized profusely. After all, open as I may be, I was unaccustomed to such physical contact in the stands. Assuring him that it was more than OK with me, we sat back down in our seats while everyone else filed out of the arena. A little embarrassed, he said he had an in with the team and asked if he could make it up to me by taking me into the locker room. Trying not to fall all over my tongue, which I'm sure must have hung down to my ankles, I graciously took him up on his offer, and off we went. Winding our way through the crowd, I didn't have a chance to ask him anything and just followed along close behind. Then we hit the locker room, and oh, my God, the men! Ranging in age from early 20s to late 30s, uniforms half off to buck-ass naked, toweling dry or shaving in front of a mirror in a way too small towel. What a sight!

We made our way up to a locker labeled CROMWELL. It was the one used by Eric Cromwell, who scored the winning goal. He was facing his locker and spun around when my neighbor called his name. He stood with shoulders a yard wide and heavily muscled. He had pecs that danced as his arms moved and a ribbed abdomen split in half with an uninterrupted trail of brown hair that formed a perfect T circling each large nipple and diving southward beyond his navel. A towel draped around his waist, hitched slightly lower on his right side, exposed a massive thigh and titillated me as it promised to fall open with his every move. His face lit up as he greeted my newfound friend—Danny, I learned his name was—with a manly hug and handshake. Their eyes locked till Cromwell suddenly realized I was standing there, probably with my mouth wide open and drooling. He smiled and offered his hand as he introduced himself. As I shook his vicelike hand, I watched his thick wrist and forearm move as his bulging biceps flexed. Obviously not shy, he continued to face us as he dropped his towel, raised his left foot up onto the bench just to my right, and dried his butt and asshole, which caused his thick uncut cock and meaty balls to swing back and forth. I've never been one to jump into public sex, but it still took all the strength I had not to fall to my knees and feast on that ample meal.

Eric was excited about the win and wanted to party, so I eagerly accepted their invitation to join them at the arena bar. Other teammates and their companions were also in a partying mood, so the place was very festive. The drinks flowed freely as they relived in vivid detail every play of the game. As we were readying to leave for the evening, Eric and Danny had some quiet words and asked me if I was interested in continuing the party at their place. Nothing could keep me from following along with the images that were flashing in my mind.

I sat on the sofa next to Eric as we toasted him as the hero of the night. Danny excused himself just long enough for Eric to place my hand on the meat running down his leg. I leaned over and began eating his cock head through his jeans. As I slid over to kneel between his spread legs, he unbuttoned his jeans and pulled his flaccid tube and balls out to hang free. I went to work on his cock, getting my tongue into the skin hood that covered a bell-shaped head crowned by a deep, long piss slit that glistened with precome. He quickly became engorged, which made me retreat down to his balls. He squirmed out of his shirt, and as I removed the clothes from his lower half of his body, I realized that we had been joined by Danny, who stood there naked with a cock as hard as a flagpole. I sucked Danny's thick meat deep into my mouth as I stroked Eric's, sliding that skin sheath his full length from cock head to ball sac.

I soon found myself lying in a circle, sucking Eric and rimming his tight asshole as I was treated to the same mind-blowing sensations from Danny. As we wrestled and continuously found new positions, tongues found tongues, mouths found cocks ooz-ing precome, balls were sucked like hard candy, and spit found its way into hot, moist crevices to be followed by massive fingers spreading lube deep into our bowels.

Eric pulled me up on all fours as he pressed the head of his cock against my hungry hole. He slowly fed inch after inch of that flesh tube into me until his meatballs pressed hard against my dangling ball sac. He instructed Danny to kneel in front of my face and fuck my mouth as he fucked my ass.

After we'd been in that position for a while, Eric withdrew his meat and flipped me over on my back. He lifted my knees over his shoulders and pushed his throbbing cock back in to the hilt. Danny came forward into a sixty-niner with me. As Eric resumed thrusting his full length, Danny and I feasted on each other's rock-hard and dripping pricks. Our mouths reacted to the speed of Eric's pounding. Feeding each other feverishly, we all sensed the pending explosion. With a few solid thrusts, Eric pushed us all to the point of no return. My body was so electrified that their come felt like hot wax being flung onto my skin. We collapsed into a heap across the bed where we lay motionless.

I cleaned up, and after we exchanged phone numbers and promises to do this again soon, I made my way home to bed. As I closed my eyes all I could see was the flashing blue light and me as I screamed "Score!"

Remembering Richard

Andy Ohio

*I*t was the first time that year that Manhattan slipped off its winter coat and dared to dream of spring.

I was walking up Lafayette Street toward Astor Place, daydreaming, wishing I never had to return to the office; I was thinking what a great day it would be to play hooky and lie around in the park when my reverie was broken by two bicycles whizzing past. I glimpsed a shock of silver hair and those gold-rimmed spectacles, and more out of instinct than volition I called out, "Richard!"

I watched as he stopped, called to his friend to stop, and turned around to bike up to me.

"Richard? It's Andy."

"Oh, my God," he said in that distinctly raspy voice, "how are you?"

"I'm good, I'm good. What are you doing in New York?"

"Oh, I'm just here for a few days, and then it's back to Seattle."

"Wow, well, we should get together."

"Yeah, that'd be great."

He introduced me to his friend, Daniel, we traded numbers, and they were off. Good God, Richard. Thankfully, he still looked the same. The silver hair, the sparkling blue eyes, that strange raspy voice, the slightly manic and disheveled air.

I can't say he was an ex of mine; our fling was too brief for that. I can't really say much at all with any certainty. It's all just a pastiche, a blur, a whirlwind of memories of how my life once was.

This was Seattle, sometime in the early '90s, and the city was still reeling from the media onslaught that grunge had brought to town. The city may have been reeling, but it was still magical. It was a small town recently filled with youthful dreamers, bright and expectant, where people could come to invent themselves and reinvent themselves again and again without the manic professionalism of New York. Lifestyles were tried on and then discarded, new ones were invented, and a wonderful time was had by all. At least, by all who survived. But that's a different story. As for me, I had been several people already and would be several more before I left.

I had known Richard on a casual basis for several years. As performers, our paths often crossed, and in such a small town it's impossible to stay strangers. At some point, when he was developing an experimental theater piece based on the myth of Icarus, in which he had cast my then-girlfriend, we began to spend more time together, sharing our thoughts on art and dreams and magic and love.

But, of course, I wasn't gay then. I hadn't even come out as bi. And though I had been sleeping with men on and off for several years, it wasn't until I met Richard that it occurred to me that my furtive assignations with men could no longer be written off as "youthful experimentation."

Several months passed. The Icarus show came and went, and my relationship with the girlfriend ended rather brutally. I was writing and performing regularly, gaining some notoriety, but my personal life was still a wreck. My days were spent on crystal, and my nights were spent drunk on whatever beer was cheapest or free. Sometimes, just to liven things up a bit, my days were spent drunk and my nights on crystal, but it depended on who was buying and how late I had to stay awake.

One afternoon I was in my favorite bar, the Comet, drinking a beer, when Richard walked in. I don't think he had ever been in there before. But I was glad to have someone to drink with and glad to see a friendly face. He sat down with me, and we drank beers and smoked and talked. I don't know what about. Probably art, theater, dreams, poetry; probably about his boyfriend, who was on tour in Japan doing some kind of esoteric dance, probably about my ex-girlfriend, who was putting some new guy through the wringer.

The afternoon light coming through the bar's window went from amber to twilight, gray to dark black, and the bar started filling up with rowdy school kids. Richard leaned over and said, "Let's go somewhere else." I agreed.

He led me out of the Comet, up Pike Street, and around the corner to a bar called, I think, the Sea Wolf. It was one of those gay bars with darkened windows and darkened everything and a somewhat surly but attractive clientele.

We ordered two bottles of beer and walked over to the corner. We were sitting there talking when I stood up to get a cigarette out of my pocket. More by accident than intent, I stumbled into Richard, but instead of pulling back I pulled him up to me, held him, and we kissed. Then we separated, sat down, and looked at each other, each of us surprised for different reasons.

We drank for a little while longer, occasionally making out and looking at each other, not finding much to say anymore.

"Let's get out of here," I said.

"Sure," said Richard, "where do you want to go?"

"My apartment's too far. Where's yours?"

"Just around the corner."

"Sounds good."

We left the Sea Wolf and went to his apartment. When he opened the door I didn't know what to expect, but I was glad to see it was a mess. Somehow this comforted me. In the past, on the few occasions I had actually ended up at some other guy's house, it was always too neat, too organized, too coordinated for me to feel at ease. Since I didn't think of myself as gay, it felt "faggy" to be in a neatly appointed bedroom, and since I was more accustomed to dives, squats, and crash pads, a tidy apartment just made me feel dirty.

We threw our jackets and backpacks on the ground, and I flopped down on his bed and began unlacing my boots.

"You want water?" he said.

"Yeah, yeah, definitely."

He poured a big glass of water and brought it over to the bed, and as I drank it he began to take off my shirt.

Pretty soon we were both naked and rolling around on the bed: biting, slapping, wrestling, making out. I was self-conscious because, even with the lights out, even though I was still thin then, I wasn't terribly comfortable being naked in front of another man. Most of the sex I had had with men was in parks or movie theaters, in the corners of bars or in the dank basements and shadowy corners of various rock-and-roll dens of iniquity. And of all that sex, I was usually clothed and giving some guy a blow job or a hand job. I didn't like to be touched. I still don't. And because I'm not well-hung, I've always been afraid I'd disappoint, afraid I'd be rejected.

For a moment, I pulled back and shook my head, trying to think straight. I looked at Richard and looked in his eyes. He didn't look away. I half laughed, and we started to make out again. I was drunk enough to do it, and I liked Richard enough to try to get past the fear.

I started to work my way down his chest and took his dick in my mouth. He was, in fact, rather well-endowed, and his cock had an elegant curve to it. His pubic hair was shaved, a fact I remembered discussing before, but still I was surprised to see a grown man with no pubic hair. As I started to suck, he groaned and pulled out of my mouth.

"What?" I mumbled.

"Nothing, I...," he reached around to the nightstand and grabbed a condom. He unwrapped it and together we unrolled it down the length of his cock.

"Why the condom?" I said. "It's just a blow job."

"I'm HIV-positive."

"Oh."

"I've been positive for like, eight years, and I've never gotten sick or anything, so...sometimes I just don't think about it but..."

"Yeah, wow. OK."

"Does it bother you?"

"No, I mean, as long as we're safe, I don't think it should be a problem."

"OK, just, you know, let me know..."

"OK."

I put his dick back in my mouth, savoring the heft of it, feeling the curve in my mouth and its length touching the back of my throat. I had one hand on his nipples and with the other fed myself on his cock. Soon my mouth was numb from nonoxynol-9 and tasted like minty rubber, and I had to catch my breath. I lay down on my back and Richard lay down next to me. His hand drifted down to touch me, but I warded him off and rolled onto my side so that his hand was on my ass instead. I'm not sure if I meant it as a cue or was just trying to keep his hands off my dick, but he started playing with my ass. I've always liked that, but most guys act like they're in a porn movie: They start right in with the slapping and the stupid porn-movie dialogue, and I get turned off. But I wouldn't learn that till much later. Richard was the first, and he wasn't like the others I would meet, and when I felt the cold touch of lube on his warm hand, I lifted my legs so that he would face me.

Once I was totally wet, more wet than I had imagined possible or necessary, he began to slide a finger in my ass to loosen me up, and then finally, slowly, incrementally, his cock.

"How are you doing?" he said.

"Unh…"

"Is that a good unh or a bad unh?"

"Unh, good, unh…"

"Too much?"

"No, but slow, go, unh, slow."

And we found a rhythm and kept going, resting, changing positions, then resting again. To be perfectly honest, I don't remember when or if he came. I'm pretty sure I didn't. I remember making my way to the bathroom, reaching the door, and saying something that had him on his feet and rushing to me, until we were wrestling on the floor and then doing it again, me leaned up on a radiator and him supporting himself, one hand on the wall. I remember taking a shower together, smoking cigarettes, and falling asleep, hours later, with my head on his chest.

As the morning light broke through the window shades, I told him he was the first person to successfully fuck my ass. I told him that I had had one other attempt at entry, a year earlier, which had been thwarted by a lack of lube, my inexperience, and the extraordinary size of the cock involved.

He looked a little shocked at first and then said, "I wish you had told me. I mean, it's, you know, important. It should be, I don't know…"

"Don't think about it," I said. "I'm not dwelling on it. It's not a big deal; it's just, you know, something to do. It's not that important."

I made some excuse, got dressed, and went home.

Later that day he called me and suggested we get together for dinner.

We got dinner, and I think we maybe went to a play or a movie or something, I don't recall.

We went to several bars, saw people, gay boys I knew who were shocked to see me with another boy, in gay bars. Shocked, maybe, or not so shocked, maybe just acknowledging that I was realizing something they had known all along.

That night, after drinking and carousing and general drunken misbehavior, Richard came over to my place. I hope he didn't mind that it was a mess. We started messing around, making out, wrestling. We got naked, I found a condom, put it on his cock, and started sucking. He pulled out, rolled me over onto my back, and worked his way down my chest to my dick. I tried to stay calm, I tried to relax, I tried…but when he took my dick in his mouth, something inside of me broke, and I started to sob uncontrollably. First little whimpers and then big groans, and I pushed him off me, pushed him away from me, off the futon and onto the floor. I gathered the sheets around me and curled up into a ball.

The heavy crying subsided, but I felt raw, electric, exposed. I murmured to myself, to Richard, "I'm sorry. I'm sorry...it's just...it's wrong...it's wrong...it's...just don't touch me, please, don't touch me..."

I didn't know what I wanted. I didn't necessarily know where I was. I didn't know what my body remembered, what happened, whether it was just homophobia or whether it was something else, something deeper. I still don't know. But I lay there, confused, hurting, afraid that he would leave, afraid that he would stay, just very simply afraid.

"Shh..." he said, "Shh...it's OK..."

He climbed slowly back onto the futon, put one hand tentatively on my shoulder, and then the other. Slowly I turned toward him, and he held me, rocking me.

"Shh..." he said, "Shh, it's OK. It's OK. It's not wrong; it's beautiful. You're beautiful..."

And he held me and rocked me to sleep.

"So," I said as we walked up Eighth Avenue, wandering around New York, talking about all the lives we'd led in the intervening years. "Richard, tell me, do you remember if we parted on good terms or bad?"

"I don't remember. It doesn't matter. I think it was one of those, 'Oh, you like me, therefore I must run away from you' deals."

"Oh, well, I guess it's OK then."

"Yeah, it's OK."

"Good."

"Listen, I'm tired," he said, "and I forgot to take my pills. Can I just come up to your place and crash for a bit?"

"Sure," I said.

We went up to my apartment, and I got him a glass of water. He sat and took his pills. He put his hands on my chest and started to rub me. I gently demurred. "No, I, no...," I said.

I didn't know why I wouldn't sleep with him now. Part of me is more cautious now, nervous about HIV. Part of me just doesn't want to have sex with someone who's going to leave. And part of me was just tired.

"Why don't we just lie down for a bit?" I said.

"OK," he said. "You know, I still remember you crying..."

"I was hoping you wouldn't."

"Why?"

"I don't know...it's just...I was such a mess then, and it was so embarrassing, and...but...I have always wanted to thank you for being so good."

"You're welcome."

"Let's stay in touch this time."

"Yeah, let's."

And we lay down in each other's arms and drifted off to sleep.

Horsing Around

Gareth MacKenzie

I had been working part-time at Oak Ridge stable for nearly a year. It gave me extra cash and free board for my horse, Rock. I spent my evenings and most weekends mucking out stalls, grooming horses, and doing light maintenance. Sometimes I even took off from my day job just to put in more hours at the stable. One of those occasions was a hot Friday in the summer of '96. I called in sick at the packing plant and spent the day at the stables. I rode Rock in the early part of the day when it was cooler and started my chores after lunch. I went to work on the stalls and was soon drenched in sweat. The stable seemed deserted, so I felt comfortable taking my shirt off. I was surprised when a horse trotted up to the double sliding doors and a rider dismounted. It was Randy, one of the three part-time riding instructors.

Randy had caught my eye when I first came to Oak Ridge. I had never seen him with a girl, and there were rumors among some of the boarders that he was gay, but I had never been around him enough to confirm it.

I left my wheelbarrow and manure fork in the stall I was cleaning. Randy had already unsaddled his horse, Beaufort, and cross-tied him in the shower stall. I came up quietly behind them. Beaufort's ears swiveled in my direction, and I knew he was aware of my presence. Randy was not.

Randy rode English and was always dressed a little prissy for my taste, but today he was casual and wore boots, jeans, and a tight white tank top. He was bent over the faucet, adjusting the water so that it would be comfortable for Beaufort. I came up behind him in time to see a view of two perfect ass cheeks covered in denim. "You need any help?" I asked. Randy just about jumped out of his skin. He stood straight up and turned sharply with the hose still in his hand. A spray of warm water struck me across the front, drenching my hairy chest and the crotch of my jeans. "I'm sorry," Randy apologized as he got the hose under control. "God, you startled me. I thought I was alone. I'm afraid I got you all wet."

"No problem," I said with a chuckle as I ran my hand across my wet chest in what I hoped was a seductive move. "I've been wetter." Randy followed my hand as it brushed my chest hairs. He looked up at me, turned a little red, and looked away. He turned his attention to his horse and began to hose him down. I leaned back against the wall with my arms folded across my chest and watched. I made some general comments about the heat and weekend plans. Randy just muttered an occasional yes or no. Randy finished wetting Beaufort down and picked up a sweat scraper from a bucket. He began to scrape the water and loosened dirt off his horse's neck and shoulders. I took up another scraper and started on the opposite side. When we reached Beaufort's back our eyes met over the gray horse.

"So where do you hang out on weekends?" I asked innocently. "Do you go to the redneck bars around here, or do you go into Baltimore and check out the action?"

"I don't go out much," Randy answered, keeping his attention focused on Beaufort. "I usually stay at home." I moved over to Randy's side of the horse. I pretended I was rinsing the scraper off with the hose. Randy's back was to me as he ran the scraper over Beaufort's rump. I decided to take a chance and lay all my cards on the table. I stepped up quietly and placed both hands on Randy's waist. He stiffened and stood still without moving a muscle or making a sound. I leaned against him. My moustache brushed along his neck. My lips barely touched his smooth skin. Randy took a deep breath and then let it out with a sigh. My hands ran up Randy's sides and around his body to his pecs. His nipples were hard beneath the cotton tank top as my palms rubbed against them. My fingers slipped under the edge of the tank and gently pinched Randy's nipples. He leaned back into me, his ass pressed into my wet crotch, and I felt my cock move with desire.

I kissed Randy's neck, and he moaned. He turned around in my arms to face me. Randy's mouth found mine as his hands slipped behind my head and he pulled me close. His lips parted for my tongue, and I explored his mouth. He kissed me like a thirsty horse sucks water. I think he needed it as much as I did. His hands slid down over my chest, massaging my pecs. I pulled him closer to me, my hands cupping his ass cheeks. I squeezed them as I ground my hips into his crotch. I slipped my hands under his tank and felt his hot skin. I worked his tank top up his body, and reluctantly our mouths parted so that I could pull it over his head.

We stripped. I never took my eyes off Randy as I pulled my boots and then my jeans off. As Randy revealed his body to me, I saw pale skin covered with dishwater-blond hair on his arms and legs and a nest of hair where his dick sprouted. My own body was dark and weathered from the waist up, and my hair was bleached almost white from the sun. When he was naked I reached out with tanned hands and pulled his smooth body into the circle of my arms. My prick throbbed against Randy's thigh as I felt the heat that emanated from his bare flesh. My mouth and hands were insatiable. Randy leaned back against Beaufort's side. The horse never flinched, never flicked his tail; he merely supported Randy as my lips and tongue ran over his chest.

I licked at Randy's nipples, my tongue circling around the areolas, wetting the sparse blond hairs that grew over his pecs. My lips closed over his hard left nipple. I sucked it and gently chewed it with my teeth. Randy's arms were stretched out along Beaufort's spine. One hand gripped the horse's mane, and I imagined Randy's fingers tightening in the gray-and-black hairs as I chewed and sucked on his tit. I released the nipple, and my tongue slid down Randy's chest and tight belly to his cock. I knelt in the shower stall on the concrete floor in a puddle of dirty water, the smell of horses and leather filling my head. I nuzzled the thick pubic hairs around Randy's slim, uncut dick. I took his meat in one hand and rolled the skin back to reveal a bright pink head. Precome seeped out of Randy's piss slit in one, two, three clear pearl drops. I lapped them up with my tongue, then kissed the cock head. My lips parted and slid over the bulging pink flesh and down the shaft. I held Randy's hips in a firm grip as my lips rode up and down his cock.

"God, Mac," Randy whispered. "A-a-ah, it feels so good. Please don't stop, please don't stop, man. I never thought…a-a-ah." Randy's whispering became an unintelligible whimper as I continued to caress his cock with my lips. My tongue ran along the underside of his penis and over his tight ball sac. I sucked each testicle into my mouth, first one round orb, then the other. I rolled them around in my mouth, tasting their sweat and musk.

My hands squeezed Randy's ass cheeks as I sucked his dick. My fingers moved down between the crack of his cheeks and played with his hole. I could feel it twitch with excitement as my fingertip pressed against his puckered hole. Touching Randy's ass brought a beautiful image of his tight butt to mind. Reluctantly I let his cock slide out of my mouth. I kissed the tip, tasting precome, before I rose from my knees and turned Randy around. Randy's eyes grew wide with uncertainty.

"Don't be afraid," I crooned like I was calming a frightened horse. "I won't hurt you," I promised.

I hoisted Randy up so that he could lie across Beaufort's back. Again the animal stood patiently and let us play. Randy's ass was at just the right height. I spread his cheeks, and his asshole winked at me like a mare teasing a stallion with her warm, moist slit. I ran my tongue between Randy's ass cheeks along his crack. He tasted sweaty with a faint leather flavor. My tongue passed over the puckered ring of muscle surrounding his tight hole. Randy quivered, and his ass muscles clenched. I licked his hole again, and then probed it with the tip of my tongue. In this new position Randy's cock was pressed against Beaufort's side and pointing down to the floor. I could see his ass, his balls, and his cock. I ran my tongue over his hole and down his crack to that smooth stretch of skin between his ass and the stem of his cock. I swirled my tongue around and continued over his ball sac and down his shaft to catch another pearl drop of precome.

I did this over and over, my tongue running from asshole to cock. I squeezed and patted the round butt and covered it with caresses. I spread spit and sweat from hole to piss slit. My own cock ached with the need for release. Precome dripped from my foreskin in a long string of clear glue. I gently guided Randy down off Beaufort's back. He turned his head to look at me as I pressed the head of my dick against his asshole.

"No, Mac, not inside me," he said with a little nervousness in his voice. "Not yet, not without—"

"It's OK," I assured him, interrupting him. "I won't go inside you, I promise, not without protection. Just let me rub."

I stroked my cock, rubbing the head against Randy's hole. His ass was wet and lubricated with spit and sweat. My rod slid along his crack with ease. I began to hump him. My cock head popped up between his butt cheeks at the base of his spine and slid back down along his crack. I reached around Randy and massaged his stiff pecker. He leaned back against me, one hand reaching behind him to pull me closer, the other clutching at Beaufort's mane. He made a fist in the tangle of horsehair as I worked his meat.

I kissed Randy's neck and ear as my hips slapped against his butt. I worked my rod along his crack as my hand stroked his cock. My other hand held him tightly against me. I wanted his ass, I wanted to fuck him, but I knew there would be other opportunities for me to have all of him.

Randy moaned and called my name three times as his body jerked against me. I felt his cock swell as he shot his load. It spurted a gooey white string along Beaufort's left foreleg. Randy's body shook with pleasure as he emptied his balls.

I released Randy's cock. My hand was slick with come, and I applied it to my own meat and worked my foreskin back and forth. Randy turned around in my arms and faced me. We still held each other as my palm rode along the shaft of my cock. I opened my mouth to cry out, but Randy covered it with his own. My cry was lost inside Randy as my cock exploded.

Hot, white gravy shot straight up from my cock head. Some landed on my chest and was crushed between us. The rest fell back onto my fist as I worked my rod like a piston. My body jerked in spasms of relief.

We clung to each other, not wanting the moment to end. We kissed until our bodies cooled and the sperm pressed between our bodies had turned to jelly. We rinsed off with the hose and finished cleaning Beaufort. He seemed to have no concerns other than getting out to pasture.

"I didn't expect this," Randy said shyly. "I mean, I suspected you might be gay, but I never imagined you would be interested in me."

"Are you kidding?" I said with surprise. "I noticed you the first day I came here. I would have jumped you then, but I wasn't sure what your story was."

"Now that you know," Randy said tentatively, "will we get to do this again?"

"We've got a long, hot summer ahead of us," I grinned, "and I've got no other plans."

"Then let's make some plans for tonight," Randy suggested with a certain gleam in his eye, which made me remember what I wanted to do to his ass.

Sean L. Avery

Several years ago, when planning my eventual escape from the chaotic Big Apple, I spent a weekend visiting the home of Paul Revere, the perpetually doomed Red Sox, and the Boston Marathon. I had originally planned to stay with my brother but upon arriving in Beantown was informed that he and his girlfriend had come down with the flu and I would thus have to find alternative accommodations. Not knowing of a place to stay, I checked into the YMCA on Huntington Avenue, figuring it was cheap and hoping that perhaps something fun might happen!

I spent the next day—a typical bitterly cold New England Saturday—checking out the sights and sounds of Boston, discerning whether or not this little village would make a good home after hanging my hat among the bright lights of Manhattan. During my stroll through the Back Bay, I picked up a copy of *Bay Windows*, the local fag rag, at the gay bookstore. In it I found an ad for a dance club that had just opened. The new disco was a second incarnation of the infamous Buddies, one of Boston's most popular gay establishments in the early 1980s.

I recalled with amusement my first boyfriend's pressuring me to move in with him—the thought making me feel more like a prisoner than a lover—and my subsequent flight from the nation's capital to Provincetown that Fourth of July weekend so that I could "think things over." I'd made a pit stop in Boston to visit my brother—a staunch heterosexual living in the queer south end—and we attempted to go dancing at Buddies after dinner one night. However, being the underage chicken I was at the time, I was refused entry, to my great disappointment. Thus, it was with much anticipation that, now being of legal age, I got dolled up in my dumpy room at the YMCA in anticipation of checking out the new Buddies, having never been able to experience its original splendor.

The club, open just a few weeks, buzzed with the excitement as everyone knew it was the hot new place to be and be seen. Indeed, Buddies was packed with the city's finest. Boston holds a reputation for being home to some of the nation's most handsome men, and the crowd that night did little to dispel that reputation. The dance floor upstairs was packed with men dancing shirtless, their muscular bodies glistening with sweat. The atmosphere was sexually charged. *Not bad for Boston!* I thought to myself, being a bit of a club snob from New York, used to huge dance palaces where the prettiest faces were picked from the masses at the door in the most fascistic behavior. Although the crowd was indeed stunning, there was also a stench of attitude in the air, which I would soon learn was, unfortunately, part of the Boston gay mind-set.

Today, having lived in Boston for a decade, I know only too well that gay men in this puritan town are very much concerned with appearances. Unlike New York or San Francisco, where it's really no big deal to be seen sucking cock in the bushes or fucking ass in a sex club, a rather conservative ethic dictates behavior in Boston, particularly when it comes to sex, and especially among gay men. The gay bars, clubs, and restaurants of Beantown are more for posing than actually picking up tricks. It's during the wee hours of the morning that the carnal nature of gay Boston manifests itself. The phone-sex lines heat up with horny men looking to hook up and shoot their loads, and outdoor cruise areas such as the Fenway Gardens and Charles River Esplanade swarm with randy dudes looking to suck and fuck (at least during the warmer months).

Being from New York, I didn't realize that such was the way of the little New England town I would soon call home. Thus, I left Buddies that night feeling incredibly sexually charged up yet not knowing where to get off. I returned to my seedy room at the Y and lay on the bed, flipping through the pages of *The Phoenix*, an artsy publication boasting a highly entertaining adult section of personal and escort ads. Feeling frustrated and horny, and being in a foreign town, I even considered ordering in a hooker.

I decided not to waste the money (I'm usually ten times hotter than any of the rent boys I've met) and thus got ready to hit the hay. I went to the bathroom down the hall to take a piss and brush my teeth and, much to my pleasant surprise, found myself standing next to an incredibly hot guy at the urinal. I said "Hello," he nodded, and my heart started racing just looking at this unbelievably beautiful specimen of man. He was tall, at least 6 feet, with a chiseled face and high cheekbones. He had short brown hair and obviously was not American. I figured, because of his light complexion and piercing blue eyes, that he was probably from one of the Scandinavian countries. He was wearing only a pair of sweatpants, and his body made even the dancers at the club pale in comparison, as he was naturally smooth and ripped with muscle. I tried to play it cool as I finished cleaning up and went back to my room.

If I'd been feeling a bit randy before, I was climbing the walls after seeing that guy in the bathroom. There I was, in my little room at the YMCA in Boston, and somewhere on the floor was one of the hottest men I'd ever laid eyes on! Horny beyond belief at this point, and figuring I really had nothing to lose, I opened the door to my room and began masturbating in front of the mirror, looking at my own smooth, tight body and big uncut dick, hoping that perhaps the guy from the bathroom might walk by and I could get something going. I was like a cat in heat, feeling like I had to get off. I stroked my cock faster and faster, using the foreskin as lube. Suddenly, the hot guy from the bathroom walked by, looked in at me masturbating, shook his head disapprovingly, and went into his room—which happened to be right across the hall from mine. Although he didn't say a word, I did notice that his gaze fixed ever so briefly on my fully erect penis.

I stopped jerking off, wondering if there was even the slightest possibility that this dude might be game. I just kind of lay on my bed for a while, keeping the door open, and seeing if he would respond at all. Nothing. Damn! Feeling desperate at this point, I went across the hall and knocked on his door. He came to the door and just stood there. "Hey, what's going on?" I asked, wearing just a pair of shorts. He'd obviously been sleeping, because his hair was messed up. "I was trying to get some sleep," he replied.

"You wanna hang out?" I asked pathetically, trying to cajole him into some action. "No thanks, man," he replied and gently closed the door.

Resigning myself to the fact that nothing was going to happen with this hot man—but keeping a load in my nuts just in case—I went back to reading the newspaper, now even more charged up and frustrated than ever. This was without a doubt one of the most sexually provocative situations I had ever encountered. There I was, horny as all hell, and just across the hall from me was this incredibly beautiful man who had witnessed me masturbating and was now in his room just lying there.

About 15 minutes later the door across the hall opened and the hot guy walked back to the bathroom. I kind of felt like something was up, but this time I just played it cool. When he came back to his room, he popped his head in the door and said, "Did you get off yet?" My heart started racing.

"Not yet, dude," I replied.

"You wanna come over?" he asked.

My heartbeat accelerated as I thought to myself, *Damn, I just hit the fucking jackpot!* I followed him into his room and closed the door.

I rarely feel nervous when it comes to sex. I was at that moment, though, probably because I knew this guy wasn't gay but rather just a horny bugger wanting to get off. We didn't say a word. He stood in front of me in his sweatpants, and I dropped to my knees. As I put my hands on his bulging crotch, my heart was racing so fast I thought I was going to have a heart attack. I felt like a teenager about to have sex for the first time. There was something very naughty, very forbidden about what was about to happen, and we both knew it. Slowly, I removed his sweats and found a pair of tight gray bikini briefs underneath—a major turn-on for me dating back to high school when my best friend and I would jack and suck each other for hours after school. My adolescent buddy was French and always wore bikini briefs, which thoroughly accented his big dick. Ever since, I've had a major underwear fetish.

So there I was at the Y that cold winter night and Mr. Gorgeous is already semierect. I began massaging his penis in his underwear, licking his legs and thighs. He just stood there occasionally moaning. I could sense that he was feeling rather awkward and not at all comfortable with what was transpiring, trying to fight his desire despite an emerging erection. I felt his cock swell up inside the briefs, and a small spot of precome stained his underwear. I delicately pulled down his briefs, releasing a fat nine-inch prick standing fully erect in all its glory. I put his penis in my mouth and began slowly sucking on it. He moaned in pleasure. I took my own eight-inch uncut cock out of my underwear and began jacking myself off while sucking on his big European prick. I felt like such a naughty little boy doing something wrong, but I was so incredibly turned on by this man that my sense of shame just turned me on all the more. As I kept sucking his huge cock, he rolled his eyes and moaned. "I've never done this before. I have a girlfriend," he admitted, trying to rationalize his behavior.

After a few minutes we moved over to the bed, where we got more comfortable, and I continued to suck his monster cock. "That feels great!" he uttered. I could tell he was still uncomfortable with what was going on yet thoroughly enjoying having his big penis slurped on. I caressed his hard, muscular, smooth chest, appreciating it only as another man could, which was getting him totally turned on. I sensed he was now relaxing a tad, feeling just a bit more comfortable. Suddenly, as though possessed, he grabbed my cock and began using my foreskin to masturbate my big prick. We sat cross-legged, both jerking on each other's huge penises. We looked into each other's eyes as we continued to masturbate one another, using our foreskins to stroke faster and faster. We were both getting ready to squirt at any second. We squeezed harder and jerked faster and faster. He sprayed first, dumping a huge load that shot all over my chest. Seeing his huge prick shooting made me spray, my come flying into the air. We both collapsed on the bed, thoroughly drained.

Neither of us said a word. We just lay there, both completely spent, for about 15 minutes. Eventually, we began chitchatting, even though it must have been about 4 in the morning by then. His name was Marc, and he pulled out a portfolio, sharing with me that he had just arrived the night before from Denmark, where he was a lumberjack prior to being discovered and signed with a modeling agency in New York, where he was headed in a few days. Although I never saw my Scandinavian friend again, every time I drive by the Y on Huntington Avenue, I smile and hear the Village People singing, "It's fun to stay at the YMCA!"

Anything

mike mazur

I met him at an adult bookstore in the summer of 1980, the day before I was to leave my western Kentucky home for graduate school in Texas. Cruising had been a waste of time that night, especially since I'd had my eye on an older gentleman who wasn't paying much attention to me.

He was a couple of inches taller than me, which made him about 6 feet tall. A head full of hair so black I thought it must be dyed sat atop a face that was pleasant if not handsome. He wore rimless spectacles that made him look distinguished, and his large arms and slight paunch were both turn-ons.

I stood outside his booth's open door, waiting for an invitation that never came. He didn't seem uninterested, but I decided he wasn't going to make the first move, so I walked into his booth, closed the door, and gently rubbed his crotch.

"Hmm," he moaned softly. "What are you into?"

"Anything," I panted, getting turned on by what was growing inside his polyester pants.

"Anything?" he repeated. "Are you sure?"

"Sure," I said.

"Do you like it rough?"

"Sure." I liked to get wild and didn't mind if a man's hand reddened my ass a little before his cock fucked it.

He asked if I'd like to go back to his hotel room. I kissed him in reply, and he didn't pull away. I refuse to get horizontal with any man who isn't willing to kiss me. He walked out of the booth, and I followed him, keeping a discrete distance.

"Why don't you follow me in your car?" he said in the light of the street lamp outside the bookstore. "We might be a while, and I wouldn't want your car to get towed."

A short time later, I pulled into the parking space next to his at one of the many rent-by-the-hour motels along the major highway running out of town. I started to follow him into his room, but he gave me his car keys and asked if I would get a bag out of the trunk of his car. It was a black leather case with a small lock on the hasp; it was heavy, and things shifted inside it as I swung it out over the trunk.

When I got to the room I gasped as I opened the door. He was naked, his cock jumping spasmodically as it rose. It wasn't overly long, but it was fat and uncut. I love uncut cocks, and my mouth began to water.

"Out of your clothes, boy." I didn't know then that I was a slave, but I knew an order when I heard one. I quickly unbuttoned my shorts and pulled my T-shirt over my head, kicking off my tennis shoes as I walked toward him.

He made me lie on my back on the bed, my feet facing the headboard. He told me to stretch out as he went to the leather bag, keyed the lock, and brought out a thick strand of white cotton rope. He tied one end of it to my right leg, pulled out the slack, than ran the other end around the leg of the bed, tying it off tightly. He pulled out more ropes and repeated the action until I was tightly spread-eagled on the mattress. My cock was standing straight up in anticipation.

"I'm giving you one more chance to tell me if there's anything you don't like."

I found it difficult to make sound, but I managed. "Anything. Do anything."

"I will." He turned to the bag again and brought out a long strip of cloth, which he wound around my head, gagging me. Then he went into the bathroom, and I heard water run for a long time. He returned with a straight razor and a towel dripping hot water. He gently placed the steaming towel on my chest and abdomen, and I squirmed in discomfort.

"When I get through with you, your skin is gonna be as smooth as a baby's ass."

I moaned beneath the gag, and he laughed. "If you don't like that, well, all I have to say is, I asked."

I had never been shaved before and didn't really understand the turn-on, but as he spread shaving cream on my chest, I think he sensed my curiosity because he looked up at me and said, "Wanna watch, boy?" I nodded, and he pulled a pillow under my head. I had a decent view of the landscape of my chest and stomach and watched in mute fascination as the hair those areas disappeared under the razor. He had done this many times before, he told me as he worked, mostly on young men who didn't want it to happen. "But then, I've never come across a boy like you. When you told me I could do anything, I knew you meant it." He looked up from his work, and I nodded again. He smiled, and my cock jumped.

When he finished shaving my stomach, he toweled me off and inspected his work, going back to remove stubble from a few places. He took the towel back to the bathroom, then returned to open a small hard-sided suitcase that had been sitting on the dresser. The case contained a portable bar, and he mixed himself a drink as I watched him. I had never been neglected like this before; sex had always been an event that started and didn't stop until it was over, but the fact that he was ignoring me began to work on my head, and my cock got so hard I thought I was gonna come. I began to writhe on the bed, my cock slashing back and forth across my pelvis as I tried everything I could to attract his attention. He watched my reflection in the mirror, I think, but refused to look directly at me, turning at last to go back to the bathroom. I heard piss hit porcelain, then silence. I began to whimper, but he soon came back with another hot, wet towel and began to lather up my crotch.

When he pulled out the razor again, I fell still. My crotch was going to be easy but my cock and balls were much harder to shave, he explained, so I would have to be really still, no matter what happened. I let my body go entirely limp, and he looked up at me and smiled again. My cock jumped again, and he said, "Stop that." I nodded and closed my eyes.

The next five minutes were as painful as they were enjoyable, as he pulled my balls up and away from my body to get the skin smooth for shaving. I winced in pain but to be treated like that felt very, very good. He twisted my cock at the base to reach around it with the razor and I almost passed out in pleasure. He sensed this and became merciless with my hot, tender skin, stretching it out to shave as far down between my legs as he could reach, pulling my cock and balls brutally to one side, then another, as he worked on each thigh. I was in agony, but I was also on the verge of coming. If he had caressed the underside of my cock head just once, I think I would have hit the ceiling with my sperm. But he was careful not to touch the head, and I began to hate him just a little for it. My balls were begging for release.

Finally, he was finished, and I thought I might get to breathe through my mouth again, but he said, "Now for your ass." He untied my left arm and leg and made me roll over to grasp my other hand. He untied my right leg, quickly looping the rope around my left leg and tying it tightly, as if he thought I might actually try to escape. He did the same with my right wrist, then helped me flatten myself out on my stomach, moving the pillow from my head to my crotch. As I lay down, my butt was now sticking up in the air, ready for whatever he wanted to do to it.

He shaved it, of course, taking his time to carefully clean the stubble off my ass cheeks. It was obvious that he enjoyed this. The act of shaving me seemed to be a major turn-on for him, and I found myself getting off on his excitement.

He finally cleaned me up and returned to stand at the foot of the bed, his hard cock staring me in the face. He knelt to gently untie and pull the cloth from my mouth. He gave me a second to work up some spit, then slid his cock halfway down my throat. I whimpered in need, and he knelt on the edge of the bed, pulling my head up by the hair to shove as much of his cock down my throat as would fit. Tears filled my eyes, and I gagged, so he relented for a moment, then shoved down again. I took more, but he was pressed firmly against the back of my throat, and we both knew he wasn't going any farther that way.

He let go of my hair and stood up, and I wiggled my ass again. Reaching for the lube, he said, "Want that ass fucked, do you?"

"Yeah, fuck me."

"Fuck me, what?"

"Fuck me, sir."

"Fuck me, sir, what?"

I wasn't exactly sure but ventured a guess. "Fuck me, sir, please?"

"In a minute." He reached into that leather bag again and pulled out a butt plug, greased it up with some lube, and reached behind me to work it slowly into my hole. I moaned, unable to form words.

A hand landed on my ass with such force that I cried out in surprise. He bent over and hissed in my ear, "Do that again, boy, and this time I'll tape your mouth shut." Another, harder slap landed, and though I tried to remain quiet, it felt too good.

"A-a-ah," I gasped, and he was instantly at my head again, stuffing the entire length of the cloth back into my mouth and reaching into the black bag for a thick roll of surgical tape. Soon, thick layers of tape covered my mouth. I trembled in lust and in sudden fear. It wasn't until that moment that I began to really think about what was happening to me—that I was tied to a bed in a motel room by a man whose name I didn't know and that this man was really going to do to me whatever he wanted. I hadn't thought about the inherent danger until that moment.

He may have sensed my shift in attitude because he whispered in my ear. "Don't go to sleep on me, boy. You know you want this. Just think, now you can make as much noise as you want, can't you?" He reached for his pants, and I actually felt goose bumps rise on my back and arms as I saw his thick leather belt slide out of its loops. He doubled it over, then disappeared from my range of view.

The first blow was almost gentle, but soon I was biting down on the cloth in my mouth to keep from screaming. He really laid into my back and ass, and some rational part of my mind began to wonder how I was going to sit in the car the next day. He didn't quit until he was panting for breath and I was sobbing freely and despite the gag drooling so copiously that the cloth in my mouth was soaked. Nevertheless, I muttered garbled thanks over and over as he eased the butt plug out of my ass and lubed his cock.

"Get ready, boy. I'm takin' a ride," he said as he knelt between my legs. Feeling his thickness bump against the back of my ass, I raised my pelvis to help him in, and he muttered, "Well, well, the little bitch wants it, doesn't he?" I groaned and nodded, still sobbing, my ass in red agony from the whipping. "Well, here," he said and shoved the entire length of it into me.

My back arched instinctively, and I came into the pillow, but he didn't seem to notice as he crashed down on top of me and began to fuck my ass so hard I thought he might actually rip the skin. He finally slowed his pace and surprised me by whispering in my ear, "I know you came, boy, but I don't care. I'm gonna fuck you for as long as I want to. You got a problem with that?" I shook my head violently, my hole already feeling good as he plowed in and out of it.

He fucked me for an hour, at least, pausing occasionally to re-lube or to take a sip of his drink. Then he would return, always fucking me in a slightly different manner. He would be brutal, then gentle, alternating short jabs with long, deep thrusts, or he would fuck me with the plug, stretching my hole again and again with the its thick center. Finally, I heard him mutter to himself that it was time to "come all over this bitch," and he pulled out of my ass so abruptly that I felt a small rush of air into my hole before it closed. In a few seconds hot liquid dripped all over my tender ass, and I bucked as each drop seemed to burn my already hot skin.

When he was through he stretched out on top of me, sliding around in the goo on my back as he slowly untied each hand, rubbing my wrists to get the circulation going. Then he got on his knees and untied my feet, repeating the massage. I slowly moved out of the spread-eagle position I'd been in for the last two hours, letting my muscles rediscover freedom at their own pace.

He asked if I wanted to shower, and I staggered into the bathroom behind him. I saw myself in the mirror and was stunned at my appearance, but I didn't lose it until he took me in his arms under the spray of the shower and kissed me. I dissolved into tears, sinking to my knees in front of him. He knelt and held me wordlessly until I stopped sobbing, then pulled me to my feet and made me wash him and myself clean. He stepped out of the shower and made me dry him with one of the rough white towels; then he took me back to his bed, tied me down, and fucked me again. I had two more orgasms before he came again. I finally dragged myself out of his room well after midnight, a full four hours after we'd entered it, and never saw him again. It was the most intense sexual experience of my young life.

Contributor Biographies

A.J. Arvveson is an aerospace engineer living in sight of El Matador Beach, just north of Malibu, Calif. "The Driver" is his second published story. Arvveson's first story, "Christmas," appeared in the Alyson collection *Straight?*

Steve Attwood is a Christchurch, New Zealand, journalist working for the New Zealand AIDS Foundation. In addition to his published news writing, he has had children's short fiction published and is working on a teenage novel for a New Zealand publisher. His main ambition is to sell a recently completed portfolio of gay short fiction and complete a gay-themed novel that has "been in progress" for the last three or four years.

Sean L. Avery is a writer living in Boston, Mass.

Wes Berlin has published short stories and erotica in various gay publications. He is working on a full-length novel tentatively titled *Men Are Like Trains, One'll Be Along in a Minute: The Secret Confessions of a Gay Sex Addict.* His E-mail address is rimshot99@hotmail.com.

Trevor J. Callahan Jr.'s fiction has appeared in numerous magazines and anthologies. He lives, writes, and plays in southern New England.

Bob Condron's first novel, *Easy Money,* was published in the United States and Canada in 1999. His short stories have appeared in the likes of *Bear* magazine and anthologies such as *Bar Stories, Chasing Danny Boy: Powerful Stories of Celtic Eros,* and *Quickies 2.* His work as writer-director for fringe and community theater has been performed in Ireland, the United Kingdom, and the United States with notable success. He lives and works in Berlin with his Irish husbear, Tommy.

Jason Di Guilio lives and writes in rural Vermont's Northeast Kingdom. He is a graduate of Goddard College's MFA writing program and teaches at a school for emotional and behaviorally disturbed youth. He continues to serve as a platoon leader and executive officer in an armored tank company as part of the U.S. Army Reserve forces.

Ryan Field was born in East Orange, N.J., in 1965. He has lived and worked in Bucks County, Pa., for the past 15 years and is finishing the final draft of a new novel.

Jeff Fisher is a novelist wanna-be living in the Pacific Northwest. His writing has appeared in *First Hand, Guys, Beau,* and *Naked Magazine.*

William Holden is a native of Detroit but now lives in the heart of gay Atlanta, walking distance from Piedmont Park. During the day William acts as an accountant but spends the late afternoons and early evenings in the park writing. During his free time he enjoys cooking and dancing at some of the hottest clubs in the city.

Donovan Lee's stories have appeared in *Campus Tales, First Hand, Hot Shots,* and the Alyson anthology *My First Time 2.* He hopes to eventually publish a collection of his erotic escapades.

Shaun Levin is a South African living in London. Most recently his work has appeared in *Best Gay Erotica 2000* and *Quickies 2.* Other stories have appeared in anthologies and journals in the United States, England, Canada, and Israel. He teaches creative writing.

Gareth MacKenzie was born and raised on a small tobacco farm in rural southern Maryland. He grew up around horses and has remained involved in equine activities. MacKenzie's erotic stories have appeared in magazines such as *Bear, Bunkhouse, Hombres Latinos, First Hand,* and *Mach.* His poetry has appeared in *The James White Review* and the anthology *Shorts.*

Michael Marsh was born in Houston. He was raised and attended school in Tulsa, Okla., and Princeton, N.J. He has been a music critic for the *Wilmington Morning News,* a contributing editor for *Oklahoma House & Garden,* and is the author of *Notes*

From Along the Path, a volume of erotic love poems. He lives in Burlingame, Calif., with his life partner, Robert Kitzman, and a naughty black kitten named Sparkplug.

mike mazur grew up in the Bible Belt in the 1960s but managed never to feel guilty about being queer. He earned a degree in music, went to graduate school, dropped out to be a full-time writer-arranger, starved, then fell into arts administration, eventually working for one of the top-rated arts councils in the nation. In 1993 he reentered academia as an administrator. He's been his daddy's boy for more than 15 years.

Lee Nichols retired as a university professor of communication studies and then moved to California's redwood coast—where he met the man about whom he wrote "The Woodsman." Before he joined the university faculty, he had been a public TV station manager, press secretary to a governor of California, and network television news reporter-commentator. He is writing his third murder mystery about Tyler Van Slyke, a gay amateur sleuth.

Andy Ohio is a writer-performer living in New York City. He was one of the editors of *The Sinner's Guide to New York* and has had his erotic writing featured in *Torso Magazine* as well as the upcoming *Best Bisexual Erotica 2000* (Black Books). He is at work on a solo performance, *Andy Ohio's Radius,* which premiered as a work in progress on June 22 at the HERE Performance Space in SoHo.

Kevin J. Olomon was uprooted from the prairie of America's Midwest and transplanted in Alaska's north country where he operates a fishermen's inn on a tiny island out in the middle of the

Bering Sea. He writes to keep from shivering while the arctic winds howl and the icy ocean crashes against the rocky shoreline.

Peter Paul Sweeney lives in Dublin, Ireland. He has published in Irish literary journals and broadcast on Irish national radio. His story "Flight" appears in *Chasing Danny Boy: Powerful Stories of Celtic Eros* (Palm Drive Publishing, 1999). "In the 1980s I hung out at a New Jersey disco named Charlie's West—revolving disco ball, sunken dance floor, raised DJ booth, poppers, the works. The amateur underwear contest inspired my story."

Edgar Wayne is an openly gay 31-year-old male. "I enjoy most anything involving the arts—writing poetry, theater, music, drawing, but I especially enjoy spending time with my family. Although this story strays from my typical writings, I like the fact that it allowed me to express a different side of myself; one I usually keep private."

B.B. Wills grew up in New York City and learned writing skills at an early age from parents and teachers who demanded the best. He relocated to Washington, D.C., where his writing skills were honed in various jobs. He experienced all facets of gay life from an early age. He likes to tell people he was born in the Bronx but grew up in Manhattan at a tender age.